Of Plays and Pals, and Pointless Mayhem

By Tracy Carol Taylor

Prince of Pages, Inc.

Arlington, VA

Tracy Taylor

Of Plays and Pals

Copyright © 2014 by Prince of Pages, Inc.

All rights reserved.

No part of this book may be reproduced, scanned, or distributed in any printed or electronic form without permission. Please do not participate in or encourage piracy of copyrighted materials that violate the author's rights. Purchase only authorized editions.

This is a work of fiction. Names, characters, places, and incidents either are the product of the author's imagination or are used fictitiously, and any resemblance to actual persons, living or dead, businesses, establishments, events, or locales is entirely coincidental. The publisher has no control over and does not assume any responsibility for author or third-party websites or their contents.

Prince of Pages, Inc.

N. Carlin Springs Road.
Arlington, VA 22203
www.princeofpages.com

ISBN: 978-1-949252-13-2
Cover Art by: Getty Images

TABLE OF CONTENTS

CHAPTER 1

It was a chilly spring day, and the gentle rain kept most students indoors. Only Rachel and Paul had ventured out for lunch.

"Hurry up, Slow Poke!" She laughed as she ran ahead.

"Hold up, Rachel. Check this out!" Paul stopped at the summer job board and looked it over.

Paul Brian Cartwright was of medium height, with a medium frame, black eyes, and dark brown hair. He was a writing student who dreamed of becoming a famous playwright. He stood outside the Drama building, reading the job listings. He searched the summer job boards religiously every day, looking for anything that could be his big break. His heart soared when he saw the advertisement that Mr. McPherson was looking for new talent.

"I'm going to be so damn famous one day." He smiled brightly on an overcast and rainy day.

Rachel was slightly miffed at being slowed down and held up as she waited for him to copy down the information.

"You done yet. I'm hungry." Rachel complained with a low growl as she leaned against the wall with folded arms.

Paul just chuckled at her. Rachel Isabella Washington was his best friend and an Engineering student. She was a medium height, but plump tomboy, healthy and full of fight. Her black hair and eyes were as dark as a raven's and hid a mind just as sharp as that raven's claws. She supported Paul in his endeavors, but she had no interest in the world of theater.

"Hey Rache', you should try this," Paul said with a smirk, pointing to a flyer on the Drama building's outdoor bulletin board.

"What? A story-writing competition? What would I do that for?" Rachel scoffed, as she cocked her head and examined the flyer closer. "Writing's your gig, not mine. I still can't believe you've got a tattoo of the masks of comedy and tragedy on your lower back."

"Hey, I like to keep my muses close to me," Paul told her as he gestured to himself.

"And I like Nikola Tesla, but you don't see me praying to him." Rachel teased Paul. "Besides, it's for the drama director Frank McPherson. He wouldn't be interested in me."

"Why wouldn't he? You tell good stories." Paul gave her a playful slap to her arm with the back of his hand. "What are you, chicken? Come on, I dare you."

"Paul, telling good stories and writing plays are two very different animals. I'll pass." Rachel told him as she walked off towards the cafeteria.

"What's the matter with you? I've never seen you run before." Paul hurried to catch up to her. "Now, I double dog dare you."

Rachel stopped dead in her tracks, turned to face him, and raised an eyebrow at him. "Never double dog dare me..." She gave him a wicked grin. "You'd lose."

"Come on, you tell great stories." Paul laughed as he faced off against her. "You know you want to."

Rachel gave it some thought as she stared him down. *There's really no reason why I shouldn't. I just love a double dog dare. I haven't a bat's chance in hell of winning anyway. At least it will be a great gag for me and my friends to laugh about later.*

"Alright, I'll do it; but when I fail, you'll carry my books and be my Guinea pig for a week." Rachel grinned wickedly.

"Heh, I'll raise you one week of servitude," Paul countered with a cunning grin. "And you'll do my science homework for the year when I win. Deal?"

"Deal," chuckled Rachel. They shook hands, and Rachel turned back. She walked up to the board and read the playwright's requirements. She borrowed a pen and paper from Paul and took down the information on the flyer. "What makes you so certain you'll win?"

"What makes you so certain that you'll lose?" Paul smirked at her.

Rachel just rolled her eyes at him. "Come on. I'm cold, wet, and hungry. Let's go."

Three Months Later…

"Rachel!" Paul's excited voice came through the door of the dorm room.

Rachel ignored him and continued working on her engineering project.

THUMP, THUMP, THUMP. Paul banged upon the door.

"Come on, Rachel!" He eagerly shouted. "Let me in. I've got great and exciting news."

Rachel rolled her eyes, put down her screwdriver, and stood up to answer the door.

"Paul Cartwright, you'd better have a damn good excuse for banging down my door." Rachel opened the door and let Paul in.

Paul smiled brightly at her. "You'll never guess who won the writing contest!" He beamed with pride and stuck his chest out.

"You did." Rachel chuckled at him. She closed the door and went back to working on her engineering project.

Paul's countenance fell, and he looked annoyed that she wasn't as happy for him as she could have been.

"Don't look so despondent." She smirked. "I knew you would. You're a great...horror writer."

"You don't like horror?" Paul walked over and stood beside her.

"I like epic stories of adventure, with humor. Real life is depressing enough." Rachel picked up her project and turned a bolt, making it tighter.

"What are you working on this time?" Paul questioned as he tried to figure out what she was building this time.

"An electromagnetic toroidal generator." Rachel held it up for him to see.

"A what?" Still confused about what he was looking at, Paul picked up her blueprints and looked them over. Then he turned the paper around and around again. "Which way is up?" He chuckled.

"If you don't understand it, put it down." Rachel laughed at him. "Now, when are you leaving for Meyerton?"

"What? Oh Yeah. At the end of this school year. I'll be spending all summer with him and learning the ropes of theater production. He may keep me on if I can prove myself to him." Paul put her plans down and walked over to her.

"Congratulations." Rachel looked up at him and smiled. "Have fun."

"Will you come and visit?" Paul happily invited her. "They've got great museums and galleries. You've gotta come. We'll have fun."

"When you stop doing horror, I will." Rachel chuckled and looked over her project, mentally inspecting it.

"Coward." Paul laughed at her. "What kind of hero are you? Afraid of a little death and murder?"

"And that's why I'm an engineering student." Rachel saluted him with her wrench.

Suddenly, there was a knock on the door. Rachel just looked at Paul.

"It's your turn to answer the door." She laughed at him.

"Fine." Paul started towards the door. "Hey, wait a minute, I won our bet."

"It was a tie. You won, and I failed, as I said I would." Rachel spoke nonchalantly, and she continued working.

"You didn't throw the match, did you?" Paul asked suspiciously.

KNOCK, KNOCK, KNOCK.

"Just answer the door," Rachel demanded.

Paul did as he was asked and opened the door. But then his eyes bulged, and his heart skipped a beat.

"Mr. McPherson?!"

"Good afternoon, Mr. Cartwright." The gentleman smiled. "Is this Ms. Washington's room?"

"Yes, sir. It is." Paul gushed. "Please come in. Can I get you anything?"

"Na, ta." Mr. McPherson smiled at him. "I just came tae speak tae Ms. Washington."

"Rachel! Come and See. Mr. McPherson is here!"

Rachel got up when she heard that she had a visitor. She dusted herself off and came to see who it was. Paul happily introduced them.

"Mr. Franklin J. McPherson, this is Rachel Washington. Rachel, this is Mr. McPherson. He is a theatrical producer and theater owner. He has produced over fifty successful musicals. He produces shows both here and abroad. His net worth is over two billion dollars in assets."

"Calm doon son, don't frighten the young lassie." Mr. McPherson laughed.

Mr. Franklin J. McPherson was a tall man with a commanding nature. His strong jaw and piercing blue-gray eyes demanded your attention when he spoke to you. Deep, powerful, and slightly accented, his voice could silence packed auditoriums with its natural authority. The Scottish King of the theater ruled his domain with a heavy hand. He captured his audience with a gentle velvet glove. He crushed his competitors with a fair but ruthless iron fist. He demanded the best from all his friends, employees, and even his enemies.

Paul pulled up a chair so that Mr. McPherson could sit down. Rachel Washington just stood before him, like a child before her father.

"Good afternoon, sir. May I ask the reason for this visit?"

"Wow, she's polite and direct tae the point." Mr. McPherson smiled at her. "I like that."

"Well." Rachel folded her arms.

"Be nice, Rachel," Paul warned her with a glare, and he sat on her couch.

"Quite right, I am remiss." Rachel unfolded her arms and gestured toward the small kitchenette. "Would you like something to drink?"

Mr. McPherson laughed at her. "Ye had a southern mother, didn't ye?"

"Aye, sir." Rachel giggled a little, copying his Scottish accent. "And my father was a Marine." She came to a parade rest stance.

"Then I'll get tae the point." Mr. McPherson stated. "I'm wantin' ye as mah protégée."

"What?!" Both Rachel and Paul gawked at him.

"But I..." Paul's brow furrowed with worry.

"I thought Paul was your protégé." Rachel finished.

"He is." Mr. McPherson nodded.

Paul sighed and sat back on the couch, placing his arms over the rest.

"Then why...?" Rachel asked.

"The title alone was enough tae laugh at." Mr. McPherson explained. "The Secrets Diaries of Baby Bear: The Real Goldilocks. It's creatively funny. I've never read anything so daft in all mah life. I like it. It's different. So, I'm going tae make ye one of mah protégées."

"Thanks, but no thanks. I'm an engineering major. I'm going to build the future." Rachel told him matter-of-factly.

Mr. McPherson sat straight up and looked her in the eye.

"Young lassie, I pride mahself on finding the best talent. Be they actors, musicians, or writers. I chose Paul because he's a damn fine writer."

"And he's an English Major." Rachel smiled and glanced at her best friend before returning her attention to Mr. McPherson. "He'll be a damn fine writer no matter what format he chooses to tell his stories in. Books, Movies, or TV."

"Ye'r are a fine storyteller with raw ability and ye'r funny." Mr. McPherson counted out her good points with his fingers.

"Gee, thanks." Rachel gave him a wicked smirk.

"Rachel, don't you realize that Mr. McPherson is offering you the chance of a lifetime?" Paul encouraged her, facepalming himself. "At least give it some thought."

"Umm," Rachel pretended to think about it. "No."

"Rachel." Paul jumped up off the couch. "Your destiny is calling you."

"My destiny is to be a Mech Tech." Rachel pointed to herself proudly.

"Ugh, you and your toys." Paul griped at her. "This is a chance for some real money."

"Excuse me, engineers make way more money than playwrights." Rachel faced Paul and stared him down. "And they better all mankind."

"Playwrights make way more money than engineers. You get paid per project, but I make royalties year after year." Paul crowed proudly, and he then smirked at her. "And we keep you geeks entertained."

Rachel rolled her eyes at him. "Paul, you are my best friend, but your pride and greed will kill you one day."

Paul blew her off. "And you're going to be the first little old lady with a house full of robotic cats."

"At least I won't have to feed them or clean up kitty litter." Rachel laughed.

Mr. McPherson watched their exchange like a heated tennis match. Then he stood up and prepared to leave.

"I've decided." He announced.

"Decided what?" Rachel asked, slightly confused.

"Yer mah protégée and I'm taking ye and Paul tae Meyerton with me."

"Hell no." Rachel protested. "I've got…"

"Nothing tae worry about." Mr. McPherson assured her. "I will take care of everything." He gave her a big smile. "Good day, Ms. Washington."

Mr. McPherson closed the door and left her room. Rachel just glared at Paul.

"What the hell did you just get me into?!"

CHAPTER 2

Now, at age twenty-seven, Rachel rested her head against the back of the brown leather couch in Mr. McPherson's office as she waited for an audience with him.

"I can't believe she's dead," Rachel told herself aloud. It was as if saying it out loud made it seem more real. "What do I do now?"

She sighed, pushing the boredom and depression out of her lungs as she enjoyed the warming caress of the central heating. Without Victoria to talk to, she looked around the office as if seeing everything for the first time.

Lavish, she thought. *Yeah, that's how to describe it … Lavish.*

Ms. Amanda Loy, Mr. McPherson's secretary, had done well for herself. She had a spacious, glossy oak semi-circular desk and an executive-style leather swivel chair. Her perfectly organized and spotlessly neat desk was decorated with only three pictures. One of her family, another one was of Mr. McPherson winning his latest theater award, and the last one was of Mr. McPherson and his protégées. Namely: Victoria Cross, Rachel Washington, and Paul Cartwright.

Rachel looked to her right and saw the door through which many theater talents had come and gone. Above the door, a digital wall clock ticked off the seconds and milliseconds as she waited. The walls were decoratively covered in the theatrical posters of Mr. McPherson's most successful plays, one of which had belonged to Victoria Cross. It made the office feel like it belonged to a celebrity, and honestly, it did. Rachel hoped that one of her plays would be hanging up there someday. Looking left, she saw Mr. McPherson's hall of fame. A great big glass trophy case displayed Mr. McPherson's many awards: best actor, best supporting actor, longest running play, and top grossing play, to name a few. Again, her eyes came to rest on the picture of her, Victoria, and Paul. Rachel sighed again at the loss of her friend, but then she shook her head and chuckled to herself as she thought about how she had come this far.

"I can't believe Mr. McPherson had enough clout with the school to just change my major like that," Rachel exclaimed with a bemused chuckle. "And Paul, he was no help—the smug bastard." *Not a day went by that he would ever let me forget it. Friends since elementary, and he's still getting me into trouble. But between him and his stupid ideas, and me and my wild need for adventure and stories. We had no good sense, but we made a pretty good team.*

Having studied the office decor, Rachel now studied herself. She was dressed in one of her best outfits: a fitted white dress shirt, unbuttoned at the collar, for Dramatic Effect, as Mr. McPherson called it. Her charcoal single-breasted two-piece suit was a perfect fit, clinging to her admittedly wide hips perfectly. The jacket cinched in, giving her just the right line at the waist. Though the pants fit her hips, they were a bit baggy and were probably made for a man to wear.

Suddenly, a tall, attractive, olive-skinned, red-headed woman in her late forties strolled out of Mr. McPherson's office. She was matronly, yet exotic, dependable, sensible, and a damn fine secretary. She was Mr. McPherson's right arm. Mr. McPherson may have run a tight ship, but Ms. Amanda Loy navigated its smooth sailing. Ms. Loy enjoyed Mr. McPherson's plays, but she also enjoyed tennis, baking, and reading.

"Oh! Hello Rachel. Are you here to see Frank?" The woman paused, realized her mistake, corrected herself, and assumed a more professional appearance. "I mean, Mr. McPherson?"

Rachel sat up when she heard Ms. Loy address her. "Hi, Amanda," Rachel replied with a smile. "How are you?"

Ms. Loy grinned back at her sweetly. "I'm doing fine. Mr. McPherson is free to see you now."

Rachel got up and started towards the door, but Ms. Loy held her back. She took a tissue from her desk, licked it, and motherly began cleaning Rachel's left cheek.

Rachel rolled her eyes and gently pushed Ms. Loy's hand away from her.

"Mom…" Rachel snickered. "I'm fine."

"Uh-huh," Ms. Loy continued, slightly straightening her collar and suit. "Why can't you wear girls' clothes?"

"Because my hips are larger than yours." Rachel laughed.

Ms. Loy gave her a motherly smack. "You're a bad little girl."

Rachel chuckled lightly as she knocked, waited for a response, and then cheerfully walked into Mr. McPherson's office.

Mr. McPherson was a man to be feared and respected until you became his trusted friend, at which point you could enjoy his well-meaning and fatherly nature. He was stern but fun-loving, and the theater was his playground. He loved to create morality plays that taught his subjects, namely the audience, the right and just way to live. He saw himself as a modern philosopher who wanted to enlighten and entertain his audience.

"Good morning, Mr. McPherson," Rachel said, standing before him like a soldier reporting for duty.

Mr. McPherson looked regal sitting behind his large mahogany desk. His every fiber, down to his perfectly pressed white shirt and blue and silver striped tie, oozed upper class. He wore his expensive, tailored navy blue single-breasted three-piece suit like he was wearing jeans and a T-shirt. It looked natural and comfortable, almost like he was born to wear it. He smiled, pulling a long, shiny silver chain from his vest. The chain was connected to a glistening antique pocket watch he always wore.

"Well, Rachel, right on time, I see." Mr. McPherson had a meticulous appearance, and his close-cut hair was elegantly groomed. He took a cigar out of the box, sitting just to his right, and gestured to the chair in front of his desk. "And fur the last time, I told ye tea call me Frank." He corrected her in a thick Scottish accent. "I'm very charmed by the formality, but we've known and worked with each other fur some time now.

Besides, I respect talent and ye have git enough tae drop the t's and q's."

With a small smile, feigned humility, and a slight bow of her head, Rachel said, "What can I say, Frank? The majesty of your position in the business, as the Laird High Potentate of Producers, causes me to approach you with all the reverence and humility my poor, unworthy pen can muster. And I think you mean Ps and Qs."

Mr. McPherson joined in the hearty laugh as he motioned for Rachel to sit on the sofa to the right of his desk. It was a Broadway black vinyl sofa. Rachel stifled giggles as images of Amanda and Frank being intimate on the couch ran through her mind. For some funny reason, Rachel had begun to think of them like parents. Frank raised an eyebrow at her.

"What are ye imagining now?" Mr. McPherson asked, knowing Rachel and her imagination.

"How's Amanda?" Rachel asked, her lighthearted grin deepening to a devilish smirk. The sly twinkle in her eyes was not lost on her friend and boss.

Mr. McPherson began laughing as he cut off the end of his cigar with a gold cigar-cutter and lit it. He shook off the match and flicked it into a crystal ashtray on his suspiciously clear desk.

"Aye, she's a right bonnie lass, in more ways than one. And you shouldn't be peaking in keyholes. Besides, ye know that I never mix business with pleasure."

"Why not?" Rachel gave him a playful wink. "This couch was made for such…activities." She giggled.

Mr. McPherson just shook his head at her mirth, and then his grin faded, and he said, "But I didn't call ye here to spar with ye today."

"Well, what can I do for you, sir?" Rachel asked, and she forced herself to be more professional.

"Have ye ever heard of a novel called Not of the Same Heart?" Mr. McPherson asked. Rachel started to say something, but Mr. McPherson cut her off. "It's okay if ye haven't, few people have. The book was a flop when it came oot in 1930.

'Twas loosely based on an obscure Greek tragedy."

"What? Okay?" Rachel replied, trying to follow his line of thinking. The confusion was etched on her face in her raised eyebrows and pursed lips.

"I believe ye know where this is heading, but if not, tae save a considerable amount of time, I have bought the rights tae book. I want ye as mah protégée tae adapt the novel into a play." Mr. McPherson declared grandly.

Rachel was stunned and had to pick her jaw off the floor to speak. "Frank, I am flattered, but I...I...I."

Mr. McPherson cut her off, tapping his thick cigar into the tray. He leveled his eyes at her, and the full brunt of his Stage Presence hit her. "But nothing, Rachel, I don't have time fur false modesty. And as ye've obviously nae learned, the business doesn't have time fur it either."

"Are you sure, Frank? You want ME to do this project?" Rachel asked, her mind reeling at the honor. She could swear she was going to look down and be in her underwear...or have some freakish and horrible death. She had to be dreaming, right? Mr. McPherson was asking her, his newest protégée, the one he had hired for a fluke to adapt a play.

"Who else do I have? Poor Victoria is dead and gone, and Paul? He's good and a little mirk fur mah tastes, but he's just nae ready tae take something like this and run with it. So, Rachel Washington, yer mah rising star. Make me proud, mah lassie."

"I won't let you down, Frank," Rachel promised resolutely. "I promise."

Mr. McPherson inhaled the cigar he was holding, exhaled, and smiled. "Good." Then Mr. McPherson pulled a weathered book out of a drawer in his desk. He held the old tome gently, almost reverently, as he passed it to Rachel.

Rachel looked at the book, its yellowed, stained pages, the faded, unreadable leather cover, and the splotchy handwritten words, and wondered just what Mr. McPherson expected her to do with it.

"Here's the book. It's the only copy that I've been able to find. Read it and do that voodoo ye do so well."

Rachel was as giddy as a schoolgirl. *Finally, after seven years, I'm being given a chance to produce a play. There will be casting choices to make. There will be long nights of directing. There will be costumes and lighting...there will be writing...hours of writing.* "Thank you, Frank," she said, standing up to take the book. "You'll not regret this."

Mr. McPherson leaned back in his chair, still grinning. "Rachel, if I thought fur a moment ye would disappoint me, then this meeting wouldn't have occurred. Good day, Rachel, and when ye have a viable script, we will blather aboot ye directing the play itself."

His confidence in her was staggering. Rachel could feel how much he believed in her, and she knew she could do this.

It's just like college all over again: graduate with honors or else.

"Thank you again, sir. And, just so you know, Scottish men should never say voodoo, it just doesn't work." Rachel beamed, her smile shining bright. She felt like she'd been offered the world on a silver platter.

"Just git the job done. That'll be payment enough." Mr. McPherson chuckled.

Rachel briefly considered skipping, but she knew better than that. So, she settled for one, and only one, epic leap into the air and a shout of triumph.

YES!

CHAPTER 3

Rachel was excited when she came home. "Ryoko!" Her shout shook the house. Or rather, it was the door slam after her shout that shook the house.

Rachel removed her shoes as she took off and carelessly tossed her coat aside. She stepped into her luxury condo and searched for Ryoko. As usual, the place was spotless. Ryoko delighted in keeping a clean house. The crisp, clean colors of blue and white covered her walls, high-polished Brazilian oak wood floors stretched out before her, soft sofas of snow white beckoned her to sit down, and art of Japanese design gave the room an air of style and intelligence. Rachel gasped and was stunned into silence; even her room had been cleaned, and her clothes were pressed.

"Who presses cotton t-shirts?" wondered Rachel aloud. She spied her clean shirts hanging on the door. "For crying out loud, Ryoko even pressed my socks and put them on hangers.

Ryoko!" she called out. "Who told you to go OCD on my closet?"

"Watashi wa daidokoro ni imasu," came the soft, feminine, but busy-sounding voice.

"What?" Rachel puzzled, trying to remember the Japanese that Ryoko had taught her.

"I'm in the kitchen."

Rachel headed towards the kitchen but stopped dead in her tracks as she inhaled the heavenly scent of the garlic and basil spaghetti sauce. She would live and die for Ryoko's spaghetti.

"Today just couldn't get any better," Rachel remarked as she continued into the kitchen. "My house looks like something Mr. Clean spat up in, my laundry is done, and I just got the biggest break of my life!"

Rachel smiled as she spotted a beautiful Asian woman in an apron. Her shimmering black hair draped down and rested upon her shoulders. The woman tasted the sauce and then added a pinch of oregano. Rachel walked up behind her and jumped onto the countertop.

"Hello, Rachel," Ryoko greeted her warmly. I am glad you're home. Dinner will be ready in just a moment. Please get off my countertop. I have to cook there, you know."

"Yeah, can't have your food tasting like butt." Rachel chuckled as she got down. But she leaned against the counter as she addressed Ryoko. "I'm glad to be home, and dinner smells great."

Rachel continued to watch Ryoko cook, humming a merry tune as she waited for her dinner.

"I take it, then, that you had a good day. And what did you say about the biggest break of your life?" Ryoko asked as she dropped some thyme into the sauce.

"I'm having a very good day, and your spaghetti makes it tops." Rachel dipped her finger into the simmering sauce and tasted it. "Mmm, heaven in a pot. Italians are rolling in their graves. No Asian should make pasta sauce this good."

"Sodesu ka? So, tell me then, what has put you in such high spirits?" Ryoko asked, smacking

Rachel's fingers away as she tried for a second taste.

"Frank has chosen me to write his next play and direct it too," Rachel announced proudly.

"Oh, Rachel, I'm so happy for you." Ryoko cheered as she looked over at Rachel. But then a serious look replaced her smile. "But you know, directing is a lot of work. You'll have to deal with the actors, the set designers, and the musicians. You'll also have to aid the producers in wooing the rich patrons to support and finance your play. Otherwise, you have no play."

"Yeah, I know. But I've already got several characters in mind for the job. All I have to do is pitch it right." Rachel said, sticking out her tongue and winding her arms in a dramatic mimic of a pitcher.

Ryoko just raised one eyebrow at Rachel and smiled slyly. "You'll need costumes then, am I right?"

"As always, you're one step ahead of me." Rachel agreed; her wide smile was tainted with just a touch of evil.

"Come on, come with me. I have something to show you." Ryoko announced.

Ryoko put the sauce on a low simmer and took the spaghetti off the stove. Rachel followed Ryoko to the den. A beautiful white lace ball gown hung on a dressing dummy in the den. The lace was so tiny and intricate, so delicate and perfectly stitched. Spaced between the beautiful swirling circles of lace were tiny pearls. It had the air of an ancient queen's ball gown and the skill of a master seamstress.

"Oh-my-God, Ryoko, that dress is beautiful!" Rachel's awe stunned her into uncharacteristic silence. She struggled for more words, and she actually stuttered. "It's so...so...so...angelic. It reminds me of Asian winters in Tokyo."

"Do you like it?" Ryoko asked as she walked over to it. "I was going to wear it for New Year's, but if you'd like to use it for your play..."

"Put it on." Rachel interrupted her roommate with a sharp order.

"What now?"

"Yes, now. Please. Pretty please." Rachel pouted her lips and batted her eyelashes.

Ryoko gave a knowing grin as she moved to the dummy and prepared to undress. Rachel hurried over and sat Indian style on the oak-colored desk. She waited with eager anticipation as Ryoko undressed in front of her. Ryoko was a very beautiful girl. She was slender, elegant, graceful, and perfect, until you got down to his boxer shorts.

Ryoji was a curious Asian male, full of painful childhood memories. When he was ten, he and his twin sister Ryoko had been in a school bus accident. Ryoji had been thrown from the burning bus, but his sister Ryoko was trapped inside and burned to death. Due to incorrectly placed toe tags, they told his parents that their son Ryoji had died. Unable to tell his parents the truth, he became a girl and pretended to be his sister for them.

It hadn't been hard. He had a tall, athletic shape. He wore women's clothing well with his slim frame. Not to mention that both he and his sister wore their hair long. Maybe that was why it was so easy to become a girl. He already had a girl's frame and a girl's features. He had bright green eyes and shiny black hair. His hair was so shiny and full that as it grew longer, he became more feminine. Looking in the mirror, he saw his sister every day. And in this way, he kept her memory alive.

Ryoji also found another way to honor her. He designed dresses. They used to talk about being the only brother-and-sister team in the fashion world. They'd plan, choose fabrics, and put together great designs. Once, they even held their own fashion show for the neighborhood, which was a great success. Many neighbors had promised to come and see them when they grew up and finally opened their own shop.

However, he was still a boy. At first glance, no one would say that he was, and most never guessed the truth. But to the few who did, he was a constant source of amusement and ridicule. Only one person in his life truly understood him and his pain, and she, Rachel Washington, rose to defend him.

"What, no briefs today?" Rachel leered playfully. "You know, you look better in tight whites."

"I was feeling lazy today and went for comfort?" He answered, as his eyes twinkled mischievously.

"Nice updraft, too, I bet." Rachel chuckled.

Ryoji smiled at her as he slipped into his new dress. "You're a naughty girl." He commented coyly.

"So, I've been told." Rachel laughed.

"Come and zip me up?"

Rachel rushed forward, stood behind him, and slowly zipped up his dress. Ryoji straightened his long black hair and adjusted his dress. And once again, the illusion was complete. Despite being flat-chested, as soon as the zipper slid up the dress, Ryoji was a woman. His mannerisms and his very aura changed. He seemed to put on girlish behavior with the dress. He slowly turned around for her so that she could see. The smile on

Rachel's face told him that this dress, too, would be a great seller.

"Have I ever told you that you're the most beautiful boy I have ever known?" Rachel muttered as she admired Ryoji.

"It doesn't bother you that I design and wear dresses?" Ryoji asked, as he turned once again to face her. His voice was soft and lilting, perfect for a lady.

"Nope," Rachel chuckled, picking up a swatch of fabric, placing it on her head, and playfully walking around blind. She lifted her hands in front of her and felt her way around. Then she lifted one finger. "First, I know you're a boy," another finger was raised. "Second, I know you're not gay. Not that I'd care." Rachel bumped into the dummy and grinned. She raised another finger as Ryoko gracefully saved the dummy, catching it before it fell over. "And three, you're a damn good cook. I might mind if you weren't such a good cook."

"Rachel, be serious. People are starting to think you're a catamite." Ryoko snatched the fabric from Rachel's head and placed it back on the table.

"A what now?" scoffed Rachel, trying to remember what that word meant.

Ryoko leaned against the desk as she addressed Rachel. "Have you read the tabloids? They're trying to make you out as a Bisexual."

Rachel rolled her eyes and waved her off. "That's silly, how can I be Bi when I've never really dated anybody. Seriously, some people will believe anything that the media tells them."

"Rachel, that's not the point. You're...."

"A girl and I have a reputation to protect? Ryoko, if there's one thing that I've learned about people...," said Rachel, and she looked directly at Ryoko. "...is that people's opinions change faster than a New York minute."

"I was going to say a rising theater playwright. Rachel, I just don't want to see you hurt." Ryoko pouted, like a little girl who had lost her doll. "You'd be surprised how much one's personal life can affect their public life."

"I know that, but what could possibly hurt me?" Rachel asked, standing tall with her hands on her hips. "I'm a Superman."

Ryoko covered her mouth, held her stomach, and shook with laughter at Rachel's silly heroic pose. That was his Rachel, alright, tall, strong, and completely unshakable.

"Oh, but wait. I need to make some phone calls." Rachel rushed to grab her address book as she reached for the phone. "I can see Mac tomorrow, but I need to make an appointment to see Olivia. Oh, and James, I wonder if he's even back in town yet. I'd better call him too."

"OK, you do that, and I'll see that dinner is done." Ryoko changed back into her regular clothes. She hung the dress back onto the dummy and gracefully glided out of the room. "Don't take too long."

CHAPTER 4

The next day, Rachel went to see Mackenzie Eubank. She took out her umbrella as she left her car and placed it over her head to avoid getting wet. Yesterday had been sunny, but cold. Today, it was grey and raining. As Rachel greeted the doorman and entered Mackenzie's Luxury Condo, she wondered if it would snow before the end of the month. Rachel hummed a merry tune to herself as she ascended to Mackenzie's floor in the elevator. She stepped out onto his floor and decided to play a little trick on him. She smiled to herself as she pounded loudly on his door.

"Mackenzie Jefferson Eubank, open up! This is the police!" She shouted in her most male and authoritative voice. "Mr. Eubank, you've got three seconds to open this door before we break it down! You boys ready? If he tries anything, shoot him!"

Inside, a stunned Mackenzie Eubank quickly covered himself in a robe and headed for the front door. He jerked it open, preparing to face his accusers, when Rachel hugged him tightly.

"Hello, Mac. How are you doing?"

"Rachel?!" He gaped, stepping gingerly into the hall. Mackenzie looked around and seeing no one, he glared down at Rachel. "What the hell are you trying to do to me?!"

Rachel just giggled at him and walked innocently into his condo. "Nothing."

Mackenzie Jefferson Eubank was a womanizing lush whom the muses had blessed with the gift of music. A tall Southern Jewish man, he got his professional start in music at age nineteen, when he started touring the world with a small jazz group.

Mackenzie had a cynical outlook on the world because of its intolerance and misunderstandings. He created music to amuse himself and anyone who would listen. His reddish-brown hair and brown eyes are as soft as his music. He was a hard man to get next to, unless you were a skirt he's chasing for the evening. But for all his ruff and discerning exterior, his quick wit and sharp tongue were even worse.

Mackenzie and Rachel became friends when he tried to seduce her after one of his club gigs. She loved his music and was fun to verbally spar with. But when he made a pass at her, he found himself on the floor looking up at her. She then sat on his loins, pinned him to the floor, and said...

"Betcha didn't know little red riding hood knew karate, did ya, Mr. Wolf?" From that moment on, they were the best of friends.

Mackenzie stood in the doorway wearing a long, dark blue robe with red lapels. In one hand, he held a lit cigar. He watched her walk into his condo. And then his eyes traveled south. Rachel didn't have much of a woman in her, other than being a girl. But still watching her walk always gave him a thrill. He finally stopped leering at her when she turned and looked at him. He grinned at her, closed his front door, put his cigar in his mouth, and went to the cupboard to pour himself a glass of cognac. He took the cigar out of his mouth, only long enough to take a swig of his cognac, and then he addressed Rachel.

"What are you doing here? Not that I'm not glad to see you." Mackenzie smirked. Then he thought of what he'd like to be doing with her. "In fact, I'd like to see all of you."

"Kinda early to be drinking, isn't it?" She asked, walking into his living room.

"It's after three pm here, and just think, it's two am in Bangkok, so I'm legal." He answered, taking a puff of his cigar, as he followed her into the living room.

"Ha! You're never legal, even when you're sober." Then she turned to face him and smirked at his attire. "By the way, where are your pants?"

"At the cleaners, getting pressed," He answered, as he grinned at Rachel. "Wanna see what I keep in my pants? If not, then why are you here?"

"You're wearing underwear under your robe, right?" Rachel teased with an evil grin. It was a lewd joke, but it made Mac smile even more. "Don't tell me; they're at the cleaners, too."

"Of course, I like my shorts starched. The chaffing reminds me of you." Mackenzie retorted, and then he held his glass out to her. "Care for a drink?"

"No, I came for something else," She said, looking around at his living room.

Rachel loved Mackenzie's place. It was a living tribute to gangster style. It was like stepping back in time to the 1920s, when gangsters ruled the city in broad daylight. His living room was an homage to the Capone style. He had Floridian mango furniture with cracked wheat-colored walls, and a big shiny black baby grand piano stationed by the large rectangular living room window. That piano was Mackenzie's pride. He polished it daily and had it professionally maintained monthly. The large windows not only gave Mac plenty of light but also plenty of inspiration at night.

"I always feel like a good fellow when I visit your place," Rachel said, as she struck a pose like Al Pacino and gave her best James Cagney imitation.

"Are you a GOOD fellow?" Mackenzie asked slyly, and then he took another sip of his drink.

Rachel looked at him sweetly, feigning innocence, and then her smile turned wicked. "What do you think?"

"Ah! May the saints be praised, so you did come to keep me company, after all." He smirked, and he attempted to grope her with his free hand.

Rachel smacked it away and answered him sternly. "No, I came for Mac the Composer."

"All the pleasures of heaven await you, and you want to talk about boring stuff like work. Well, Mac the composer is out right now. Mac the libertine is in." He announced, and he mimed handing her a business card. Rachel shook her head as he sat in his favorite cordovan leather armchair. "Come, sit on my lap and we'll listen to some quality music together."

As Mackenzie sat down, Rachel looked at his CD player and listened; a Django Reinhardt tune, "Low Cotton," was playing.

"Mac, I'm writing a play, and I need you to compose the score," Rachel told him outright.

Rachel was talking, but Mackenzie wasn't listening. He was enraptured by the music, savoring his cigar and lightly nipping at his cognac. He was in another place. Rachel rolled her eyes and changed her tactics. She moved in time with the music and unbuttoned a button every time the beat went allegro. She got the first four buttons open, and then she dropped in Mackenzie's lap.

He opened his eyes. She took his cigar, oh so deliberately brushing his shoulder, and placed it in the ashtray. She then took his Cognac, making sure their hands were brushed, and took a sip. She reached across him, pressing her chest into him, and put it down on the side table. Mac grinned happily, fully appreciating her taunting bosoms in his face.

"Changed your mind, I see." Mackenzic grinned as he pulled her closer to him. Then Rachel reached inside his robe and took hold of his manhood. "Now what are you looking for?" Mackenzie asked slyly, as he enjoyed the sensation of her soft and wondering hands.

"Loose change," Rachel smirked, tightening her grip just enough. "Oh look, a roll of quarters."

"Keep that up, and it'll be a roll of half dollars," Mackenzie chuckled, appreciatively squeezing her left breast.

Then Rachel squeezed harshly and gave his manhood a good twist. Mac nearly jumped out of his seat.

"Ow! Not so rough shiksa," complained Mackenzie. "I'm not that kinky."

"Mac, I need the head on top. Not this one. Why did God give men two heads, but only enough blood to fill one at a time?" Rachel asked, with a great teasing smirk. "Do I have your attention now?"

"You've got more than that. You've got my future." Mackenzie groaned painfully.

"More than you know, Mac. I'm doing a play for Mr. McPherson."

"Mr. McPherson? THE Mr. Franklin McPherson of Broadway?" Mackenzie asked, the lust draining from his face like dripping wet paint. The brilliant light of talent and the spark of genius replaced it.

"You are working for the most famous playwright of our time?

"Yes. And I need you to do the score." Rachel said as she loosened her hold on **Little Mac**. "So... will you?"

"Yes, this could be a big break." Mackenzie's enthusiasm was palpable, and Rachel could almost feel him being pulled towards his piano... or his trumpet... or his violin.

"Yes, I know. If you can create and arrange a musical score to wrench human emotion from my audience, you'll be the new Gershwin, Berlin, or Ellington." Rachel let go of his manhood and held her hand up. She waved it to the right, gesturing Mackenzie's name in lights.

"I'm not that good." Mackenzie looked at her and thought about the possible songs he could use.

"Liar." Rachel hissed playfully. "Yes, you are. I've heard you play." She praised him.

Mackenzie sighed as he placed his left cheek on Rachel's bosom. "Yes, you heard me play solo and with my quintet at a couple of clubs and a few parties, but that isn't the same as doing a score for a big production. To be candid, I've never written anything for more than a six-piece ensemble." Then, with a slight grin, Mackenzie raised his head to look Rachel in the eye. "But for you, I promise to give you the best I have. Besides, I am getting tired of drinking off my trust fund."

"Splendid!" Rachel beamed, crushing Mackenzie in a hug. "I knew I could count on you."

"Is there a script yet?" He asked, again taking the opportunity to look down her shirt.

"Not yet, but I have ideas." Rachel pondered, giving him a wicked grin.

"Do tell," He chuckled and leaned back.

"Well, it's dramatic and sort of dark."

"Rachel, you're not a dark, dramatic person." Mackenzie scoffed at her.

"I know, but I think Frank's testing me. He wants me to fill his shoes; to do that, I must be able to do comedy AND drama." Rachel said, and Mac nodded in agreement. "Come to think of it, maybe that is why he chose both me and Paul all those years ago."

Mackenzie could feel her potential. *That's not all I'd like to feel.* He grinned to himself. "So, what's the plot of this dark drama?" He inquired.

"See, these three women are ill-used and abused by their husbands. They meet in the café of the Harridan Hotel. They are planning to get rid of their husbands," Rachel explained.

"Oh, I like it." Mackenzie jested.

"You like the plot so far?" Rachel wondered what he was thinking.

"No, your thigh. You're still sitting very nicely on my **attention**. Now, if you'd be so kind as to move a little. Bouncing works best." Mackenzie chuckled. Rachel stood up. Mackenzie frowned and reached for his drink. "Really, Rachel, getting a guy all worked up for nothing, how rude."

"Be serious," Rachel demanded, hitting Mackenzie in the head for good measure. "Where is the serious Mac from three seconds ago? Is your attention span that short?"

"I am serious," He leered at her. "How does your play end?"

Rachel started pacing while buttoning up her shirt. "I don't know yet. I'm having trouble getting there." The worry made her irritable and infused her with nervous energy. Just a second ago, she was so excited about this, but now she was just scared—scared of messing up and scared of failing.

"Yeah," Mackenzie pondered, as he reached for his cigar and took a puff. "So am I."

"Yeah, right, you've never had any trouble getting there," Rachel smirked as she turned her attention back to him. "It's getting back out again that was always your problem."

"Tell me about it," He laughed, thinking of the many crazy Ex-girlfriends he'd left behind.

"Speaking of which... How's Olivia?" Rachel asked cautiously.

Mackenzie frowned. "Pick someone else," He strongly suggested, getting up to refill his glass. "That heartless, self-serving, megalomaniac is still giving me nothing but grief."

"Really? Didn't you get a restraining order?" Rachel laughed at him as she watched his movements.

"No, and that wouldn't stop her anyway." Mackenzie huffed like an angry child before continuing, "Not only did she cheat on me, but she did so in my bed! But to make things really nasty, she has tried in every way she can to ruin me professionally. The last time I spoke with her; she tried to excuse her actions because she was mad at me." Mackenzie took another puff on his cigar, sipped his cognac, and then added in a sarcastic tone of voice. "She then offered to forgive me of all MY sins and take me back. Needless to say, I told her what she could do with her offer…. in very graphic high-definition detail."

"See, she's perfect for the role of Beatrice, the murderous wife," Rachel commented, tapping her chin thoughtfully.

"Don't give her any ideas!" Mackenzie shouted at her. The look of dread on his face was so exaggerated that it was fantastic. "Besides, she's a prima donna of the first water. If you use her, she'll make your life miserable, and she will enjoy watching you suffer."

"Well then, it's a good thing I'm really good at kissing ass." Rachel smiled at him and slapped her backside for effect.

"You can kiss my ass anytime," Mackenzie smirked and he raised a glass to toast her.

CHAPTER 5

It took a week of phone calls to reach James Farrington III. He was very successful and very busy. But Rachel finally got him to commit to spending the holidays at home with her, which was good because she had a favor to ask.

"Jamie, me boy-o! Long time no see!" Rachel exclaimed, diving into James and nearly crushing him in a big hug.

James Farrington III was not a tall man. He was short for a guy. His small frame was in constant danger of being blown away by a strong wind. His library oak brown eyes always smiled, and his laser lemon yellow hair shamed the sun. Rachel had always found him to be an easy-going, but peculiar man. And for one who was of Finnish background, he sure didn't have their strength.

Rachel had met him in college and rescued him from some college fraternity prats using him as a hot potato. There were two things Rachel could never really get used to about James. One thing was his cat, Mr. Tabby. James treated the cat like a family member, like a son. Mr. Tabby never really took to Rachel either, and only seemed to put up with her because she made James happy.

The other thing Rachel could never get entirely used to was that James was a con artist and a thief. She didn't care one way or the other about his personal life. His business was his own. But it was a strange fascination for her actually to know someone who was a professional baddie. James Farrington was a thief first and a professional interior designer second. He was the front man for a ring of thieves who prided themselves on being anti-heroes. Robbing the rich but only giving half to the poor. After all, even anti-heroes had bills to pay.

"Rachel!" James cried out excitedly. "It's good to see you again. Look, Mr. Tabby, it's Rachel."

A big black and white Hemingway cat came to see what all the excitement was about. Mr. Tabby took one look at Rachel and sneezed.

"Bless you," James says, looking down at his cat.

"Cats can sneeze?" Rachel questioned her friend. She carefully eyed the cat as she followed James inside.

"Cats can do anything," James said, picking up Mr. Tabby. "Isn't that right, Mr. Tabby?"

"And I thought it was freaky when the cat cried," Rachel commented as she entered the living room.

"Mr. Tabby is very sensitive, aren't you?" James stroked the large feline, and it purred like an expensive engine. "Mr. Tabby is very emotional."

"So's his owner," Rachel muttered, stifling a giggle.

"What?" James gave her a sly look.

Rachel smiled at him pleasantly as she entered his penthouse condo. James was a very artistic man, and his surroundings displayed this. Bright, vibrant colors adorn the walls—daredevil red, reverie pink, royal purple—and it was evident that James did not believe in calming neutrals. Modern artwork, as beautiful and quirky as James himself, decorated his home. Oddly shaped sculptures threatening to teeter over at the slightest breeze were everywhere.

"So, who are you guys knocking over next?" Rachel asked, with a mocking grin.

James escorted Rachel to his kitchen and prepared to make himself some coffee.

"You know I can't tell you that." James chuckled.

"Why don't you just become an interior designer full-time?" Rachel asked. "You're damn good at it and I know you make good money."

James stopped and winked at her. "Because thieving is so much fun."

"Alright, Dodger," Rachel told him playfully in her best British accent. "But you can't play Robin Hood forever."

James' kitchen had beautifully designed Victorian pine countertops and cabinets. It was large enough to cook for and feed an army, but he lived alone...with his cat. James made himself some coffee, and Rachel paced around his kitchen, snacking on a carrot. Mr. Tabby joined them, and James petted his cat.

"Oh, guess what?" Rachel prompted, between bites of carrot.

"What?"

"Guess who's been selected to write and to direct the next Franklin J. McPherson production," Rachel said, her grin heavily lacing her voice. James could see it without even looking at Rachel.

"You," James answered happily.

"Yep, I'm now a playwright and director," Rachel beamed, and she stuck her chest out with pride.

"No way! That's so great!" James squealed, fanning himself like a weak southern belle.

"Yeah, and I have two favors to ask of you," Rachel added, holding up two fingers.

"Oh, really, like what?" James poured a bottle of Perrier water into the cat's dish.

"One, I want you to design my sets." Rachel decreed, as she sat on one of his kitchen stools and leaned on his countertop.

"No way," James yelled excitedly. Rachel could swear that she could see James start bouncing.

"Way, and two, I need to use your place to host a New Year's Eve party. The play won't go anywhere without money, and Frank says New Year's Eve is the perfect time to pick the patron's pockets. What do you say? Can I please hold the party here?" Rachel spread her right hand to her right, indicating James' place.

"Of course, you can. Hosting a huge Broadway party for rich art patrons who may need their homes interiorly decorated...this could be a honey of a deal for both of us." James added, his eyebrows rising as ideas filled his calculating mind.

"You're right." The sarcasm dripped from her voice like a leaky faucet. "I hadn't thought of that."

Suddenly, James understood. Rachel had thought of this and was using it as an incentive to get him to say yes to hosting the party here.

"You're sneaky." James narrowed his eyes on her and grinned.

"I learned from the best." Rachel gave the cat a scratch behind its ears.

"We're not sneaky, are we, Mr. Tabby?" James said, pretending to be hurt. "We're creatively clever."

"Ha, yeah right, and I'm romantically inclined." Rachel laughed and poked the cat, making it hiss and swat at her with its paw.

"Dear, if anybody needed to be romantically inclined in the horizontal, it's you." James chuckled as he entertained the thought of Rachel in bed with someone.

"Hey! I'm just particular," Rachel said, acting insulted.

"No, honey, particular is what Mr. Tabby is." James calmed his cat with a gentle stroking of its fur. "What you are is prudish."

CHAPTER 6

It was two O'clock in the morning. Ryoko had gone to bed hours ago; and she had warned Rachel not to stay up too late. However, Rachel was still sitting at her desk, head in her hands, and staring at her computer. She was perilously close to a coffee overdose and still nothing.

The play was only half finished. She had the characters, and she had the beginning done. She had gotten them to the hotel. She had successfully knocked off two husbands, one by prescription overdose and the other by a bathroom accident. Now she was out of ideas. They had to have deaths that were plausible accidents. And they had to fit the basic model of the play. So, how was the third one to die? That's when the lights started to flicker off and on. It was like mini-lightning flashes in her room.

"What the...?!" She exclaimed, looking around. "Maybe somebody somewhere is being electrocuted. Now wouldn't that be a damn scary coincidence." Just then, the TV came on all by itself; the noise of which made Rachel jump right out of her skin. "Okay, now that is too damn freaky. Better watch it, Rachel, or you'll end up in a Twilight Zone episode."

Still shaking from the sudden fright, Rachel got up and turned off the TV. She also unplugged it, just for good measure. Then she turned around to go back to her desktop, but suddenly, there was a knock on her front door.

"Umm." Rachel's imagination ran wild. "Who could that be?" *The victim seeking help or the killer looking for someone knew. Or it could just be one of your drunk neighbors looking for his apartment. Chill out, you nutball, and open the door.*

Rachel went to the door, looked through the keyhole, recognized a friendly face, and opened the door.

"Hello, Amanda, what are you doing here at this hour?" Rachel asked as she ushered Ms. Loy into her apartment.

"I was coming home from a movie and saw that your lights were still on. So, I decided to stop by." Ms. Loy took off her coat, folded it neatly, and laid it on the couch beside her. "How is your story for Mr. McPherson coming?"

"Eh, good and not good." Rachel shrugged. "I'm only half done, and quite frankly…I'm stuck."

"I thought you might be." Ms. Loy acknowledged. "No offense, dear, but this is a Victoria-type story."

"Don't I know it." Rachel sighed heavily. She brought over a chair to sit down on and sat down on it backwards. She leaned upon the backrest as she spoke to Ms. Loy. "I miss her a lot."

Ms. Loy gave her a motherly smile. "I know you do. You two were so close."

Victoria Elizabeth Cross was tall for a girl—a giantess. Her blonde hair and blue eyes made her a virtual goddess, and she had the attitude to be one, too. She was bold and proud, with the bearing of an Amazon queen. She was a no-nonsense kind of girl, and she was smart. She hated being referred to as a *dumb blonde*. She worked hard, she played hard, and, like Mr. McPherson, she demanded the best.

Rachel met her when Mr. McPherson brought them together and immediately recognized her as someone to follow. Rachel had been taken by her strength, her determination, and her professionalism. When Victoria Cross spoke, you listened, for she never spoke idle words. Her plays were slices of life, and her characters were both real and vibrant. Watching a Victoria Cross play, you always leave learning something new about yourself. Rachel knew she could never be as serious as Victoria. She was too playful. But that didn't mean she couldn't learn to make her characters have meaning and depth and still be fun.

Victoria hadn't liked Paul. He was too calculating and manipulative for her. But Rachel was like an overzealous puppy. And for some strange reason, she liked her. Rachel could make her laugh and brighten her darkest mood. Maybe that was why she let Rachel follow her around all the time. She was her own little personal ray of sunshine. That, along with the fact that Rachel could see things in more than one way, also helped her give her characters more depth. With Rachel around, her villains were misunderstood heroes, and her heroes had dark sides that they didn't even know they had until circumstance pushed them too far.

"Victoria thought her life perfect when Mr. McPherson chose her to be his new protégée and heir to his theatrical kingdom. That was, she thought, her life perfect. Perfect until a car's headlights were the last thing she ever saw." Ms. Loy reminded Rachel.

"Yeah, I read the papers. Whoever did it didn't even put on the brakes. It was a deliberate murder, and yet they have no clues." Rachel sighed, and her eyes began to water. "If I ever find out who did it, I'll kill them myself."

"Now, Rachel," Ms. Loy smiled lightly at her. "You're not that kind of person."

"I know." Rachel gave her a very weak smile.

"That's why it surprised me that he put you in charge instead of Paul." Ms. Loy thought about it.

"Yeah, me too. I mean, this is Paul's dream. He wants to be a theater producer so badly." Rachel agreed with Ms. Loy.

Ms. Loy brightened a little. "Well, Mr. McPherson is an excellent judge of character. So, if he chose you instead of Paul, there must be a reason."

"What if he's wrong?" Rachel worried and turned her head to the side. She rested it upon the chair's back.

Ms. Loy stood, raised Rachel's chin so that she could look her in the eye, and told her. "You'll do fine. Both Mr. McPherson and I believe in you. You just have to believe in yourself."

"Maybe." Rachel gave her another weak grin.

"That's one thing I've noticed about you. You'll rush headfirst to defend others but rarely defend yourself. You're all false bravado." Ms. Loy let go of Rachel's chin and just stood over her.

"Hey, I'm a military brat. It's called cocky arrogance." Rachel joked.

Ms. Loy rolled her eyes at her. "Now, I'll let you in on a little secret about Frank. He may act gruff, but he's a hopeless romantic who likes happy endings." Revealed Ms. Loy. "Your two murderesses must be caught and punished."

"And the third one?" Rachel looked up to her for answers.

"Has a change of heart. She falls in love and rats out the other two." Ms. Loy stated.

"That's mean and unfair," Rachel whined. "After all these women endured from their husbands. Can't the third just disappear, taking the secret with her?"

"That's the movies, dear. We're the theater. We are all about morality plays. Good guys win and bad guys lose. We are the moral guardians of humanity. We show them right from wrong. We show them the rewards for virtue and the consequences for sin and vice. Got it?" Ms. Loy informed her.

"Yes, I understand." Rachel nodded. She was still trying to decide how to end her play and how to change it to accommodate this new ending.

"If your two murderesses had chosen to divorce their men, then that would be fine. But they didn't, they chose murder instead, and for the money. So now, they must suffer the consequences. The Bible says Be angry, but sin not." Ms. Loy picked up her coat and headed for the door. "Goodbye, Rachel. I'll see you tomorrow." Ms. Loy opened the door. "And don't worry. Mr. McPherson handpicked the three of you as aspiring playwrights out of hundreds for a reason. Just follow your muse and you'll do just fine."

Rachel stood and followed Ms. Loy to the door. "Yeah, have a good night, and drive safely...please."

Ms. Loy smiled at her again, gave her a simple nod of reassurance, and left.

Suddenly, Rachel got hit with an idea of inspiration. She hurried to her seat and finished her play by the end of the next morning.

CHAPTER 7

The day after Rachel finished the script, she took it to Frank McPherson for his approval. Mr. McPherson made Rachel sit in front of his desk while he read the script from the title page to the very last page. Rachel sat and waited nervously as he read it. She was so nervous that her stomach began to ache. She had never done drama before; she was just no good at being serious.

As Mr. McPherson read her play, she looked at the walls and read his academic achievements. She looked up at the ceiling and counted the nooks. She listened to the small electric fan as it cooled the room, and she listened to her heartbeat, which was faster than usual. From time to time, Rachel would start to say something, but Mr. McPherson would just raise his hand to signal her to be silent. When he finished reading it, he set the script on the desk, took a cigar out of the box, and lit it.

"Well!" Rachel demanded, as she gnawed on her first knuckle, exceedingly anxious to learn what Mr. McPherson thought of her play.

Mr. McPherson shot Rachel a cold look, "Rachel, I have read some lousy scripts in mah time, and I've even written a few. But this, mah dear, is nae one of them." He then smiled wide and continued, "This is brilliant. Yer interpretation of this novel is exactly how the play should have been done."

Rachel had a look of both shock and elation on her face, and she stopped chewing on her knuckle. "Frank, you really do like it? You're not just being kind to me?"

"Rachel, I don't waste time on compliments when they aren't warranted. Yes, I like it. This will be a triumph. It may even run for a couple of years. I knew ye could be dramatic, if I challenged ye tae be."

Rachel sank back in the chair and let out a sigh of relief. The worst was over.

"By the way, do ye have any ideas fur a cast?" Mr. McPherson asked, taking a puff of his cigar. "Or would ye like me tae make some calls fur ye."

"No, sir. I've several characters in mind for this already. I think Olivia Reed would be brilliant as Beatrice." Rachel said, sitting up to face Mr. McPherson.

Mr. McPherson looked towards the ceiling as he considered her choice. "Reed… Hmm, she is a veteran actress and a brilliant one. But she's a real prima donna. Do ye think ye can handle her?" His gaze returned to Rachel.

"Yes, sir, I have learned from you how to deal with personalities in this business," Rachel said confidently. "I have also found the right person to work the music for this production."

Mr. McPherson grinned with interest. "Who've ye got?"

"Mackenzie J. Eubank." Rachel beamed with enthusiasm in her voice.

"Eubank? I've heard him play at a couple of different nightclubs around town. He's good, but doesn't he have a bit of a reputation with the sauce and the ladies?" Mr. McPherson asked her, a bit concerned.

Rachel had expected his reservations and was prepared to support her friends. "I have known Mac for years. Yes, he's a big bad wolf with a taste for good liquor, but when it comes to his professional reputation, he defends it vigorously."

Mr. McPherson still looked unconvinced, but before he could say anything, Rachel interjected more.

"Mac gave me his word that he will give me the best he has. Mac may be a lot of things, and he'd be the first to call himself most of them, but no one has ever been able to say that he has broken a promise. And he's never broken a promise to me."

Mr. McPherson shrugged his shoulders. "Okay, if ye trust him, then it will work fur me." said Mr. McPherson, taking another puff on his cigar. "Just be certain he behaves himself and doesn't git himself or ye arrested."

"Frank, I can assure you that Mackenzie Eubank is the least of our problems," Rachel assured him.

"That's true. Ye still need a set designer, a costume designer, and rich backers." Mr. McPherson reminded her.

"I have found the perfect person for set designs." Rachel declared, with a lighthearted chuckle.

"Uh oh, who is it?" Mr. McPherson asked jokingly, as he puffed away on his cigar.

"James Farrington III." She replied proudly.

"Him?!" Mr. McPherson's face flashed in stark disbelief.

"Yes, he is one of the most sought-after interior decorators in the business." Rachel smiled and then added. "Besides, didn't he remodel your summer place in Florida a few years back?"

"Aye, he did. I'm the only man in the Keys with a Lavender Sunroom. The room is stunning when the sun hits it, but it's still lavender." Mr. McPherson rolled his eyes as he remembered the room's accents and furniture. He took another puff on his cigar and chuckled about it.

"Well, he's..." Rachel began, but Frank cut her off.

"Relax, Rachel, ye've sold me." Mr. McPherson held up a hand to interrupt her. "And yer costume designer?"

"Sato Ryoko." She answered with an elated smile.

Mr. McPherson took the cigar from his mouth and learned forward. "How did ye git her?" He asked, in stunned awe.

"Our parents share the same graveyard," smiled Rachel, her eyes flashing with mischief.

Mr. McPherson sat back in his chair and exhaled his cigar smoke. A great puff of smoke rose into the air. Mr. McPherson took a couple more puffs on his cigar as he contemplated her achievements thus far, and then he gave her his approval.

"Well, lassie, I'll leave the matter in yer capable hands. Make this a success, and ye'll be producing plays right alongside me. But I have tae ask. Where did ye git yer inspiration?"

"Pixies? No, Thalia." Rachel snapped her fingers as she remembered the name of the Comedy Muse. "Thalia's the fun goddess." Rachel snickered. Then she frowned. "I'm not like Victoria. I could never be as clever as or as deep as she was. Tell me, Frank, do you ever think about Victoria?"

Mr. McPherson's smile faded, and he replied. "Virtually every day, she could have bin a truly great producer, and in many ways, ye and she are the daughters I never had." He took a long draw of his cigar and then exhaled. "But why do ye ask?"

"No particular reason, I've just been thinking about her." Rachel stood and started walking toward the door. "Well, Frank, I need to get going. I'll see you around."

Mr. McPherson sat back in his chair and watched her leave. "Farewell, Rachel, I will see ye later." But before Rachel walked through the open door, Mr. McPherson grinned and called out to her.

"Rachel, on yer way out, please ask Ms. Loy to come in here, will ye. I need her to go out and do some errands for me."

"Aye sir." Rachel saluted him and left his office. As she passed Ms. Loy's desk, Rachel winked at her. "Amanda, Frank needs you to entertain a few of his ideas." She smirked.

Ms. Loy stood up, pulled out her notepad, and moved towards Frank's office. "That's not what he said, and you know it."

"How do you do that?" Rachel curiously looked at Ms. Loy.

Ms. Loy gently smacked Rachel in the head with her notepad, and she pushed Rachel out the front door. "I know Mr. McPherson better than you do." Then Ms. Loy turned on her heels and headed for Frank's office.

CHAPTER 8

Getting ahold of Miss Olivia Reed proved a little more trouble than Rachel thought it would be. Miss Reed was important enough to make people wait for her and work around her schedule, even when they brought her potential work. After being put off for manicures and spa treatments, Rachel finally got an appointment to see Miss Reed on Wednesday at precisely 5:30 p.m.

"My name is Rachel Washington. I'm here to see Miss Olivia Reed." Rachel informed Miss Reed's dignified butler.

The butler looked Rachel over. "Yes, I've read about you. Seems the tabloids finally got a story right."

Rachel just smirked at how she must have looked to his *superior* senses. After all, she was dressed like a boy in a business suit. After a good look over and probably many jumped to conclusions, he finally let her in.

Rachel just kept her quirky thoughts to herself. Be *careful, Malvolio. You, too, may fall hard. Trouble lies ahead for butlers who consider themselves as important as their employers.*

The butler turned and ushered her through the luxurious mansion. "Right this way, please. Miss Reed is in the arboretum."

The butler guided Rachel to the arboretum. She watched as Olivia pruned her roses, watered her morning glories, and talked to her begonias. Olivia was a beautiful harridan. Her sly doe brown eyes, long and flowing auburn hair, and **come-hither** nature had drawn in and trapped many men in her day. Seeing Olivia, Rachel could now understand why Mac would fall for her, but how he could've put up with her overwhelming need for attention and self-serving nature was a total mystery to her.

Alcohol, like makeup, must cover a lot of flaws. Rachel thought.

However, it was her need for attention that brought Olivia to the theater. It was the perfect arena, as all eyes were focused on her, and as long as she felt their eyes on her, she gave them her best. Olivia became the Queen of the theatrical world and earned the nickname Her Highness. She had the power to make or break a production. Many playwrights, like wanting suitors, showed up at her door seeking her help and blessing for their plays.

Rachel knew of Her Highness's self-importance, but as many of her actors and actresses were unknowns looking for their big break, Rachel needed a name to draw the crowds. And so, she too came to Olivia's door. Divas, such as Olivia, had to be handled with care. You had to seem subservient in their presence, even if it wasn't your nature to be. The butler introduced Rachel to Miss Reed, took orders from Miss Reed about this evening's dinner, and then took his leave.

Miss Reed looked at Rachel, raised an eyebrow at her, and then she too looked her up and down. "Nice suit." She commented in a highbrow manner. Then she turned on her heels and left the main arboretum. Rachel watched her go.

Rreow. Rachel mused as she watched her walk away. *She's worse than Mr. Tabby.*

"Aren't you coming?" Olivia called back, without ever turning around or stopping.

Olivia's order caused Rachel to come out of her silent contemplations, and she followed Miss Reed to an enclosed area of the arboretum. It was a large, glassed room with huge bay windows. It had a window box seat and a sofa for two. Miss Reed sat in a huge wicker rocking chair and asked Rachel to join her. Rachel sat on the loveseat.

"Something to drink?" Miss Reed offered, pouring herself a drink.

"No, thank you." Rachel shook her head no.

"Now then, tell me, what is this play you want me to do?" Miss Reed sipped her drink and then settled back to listen.

"It's called A Little Change of Heart. It's about three women from various backgrounds with nothing in common, except that each is ill-used, neglected, and abused by their husbands. Each goes to the Harridan Hotel for one reason or another, and they all fatefully meet in the hotel's café. Each one wants to kill her husband, but each knows that if they're suspected or caught, the insurance money is lost. So, they switch husbands. Each one promises to kill the other's husband." Rachel explained as she shifted in her seat to a more comfortable position.

"A little dark, don't you think?" Olivia interrupted her. She put her cup back down and straightened her skirt.

"All Greek tragedies are." Said Rachel. The look on Olivia's face gave her the air of boredom and an uninterested look. Rachel knew she was losing her. "But like all Greek tragedies, the players become immortal, and their roles endure for all time."

Olivia raised an eyebrow as she thought this over. She poured another drink, swirled her cup, and watched the ice cubes turn in the glass.

"Immortalized in the theater, like Helen of Troy, Mary Queen of Scots, and Carmen." Olivia pondered. What heights will this play propel my career to next? Will it become an international success? Will I become the newest best stage actress of all time, both at home and abroad?

"Exactly." Rachel smiled, sat back, and crossed her legs.

"So, what happens next?" Olivia took another sip of her drink.

"Well, two of the wives go through with it. Two husbands are dead. The third wife falls in love with her target and has a change of heart, thus the title. The two of them spend a romantic weekend in Spain. He tells her he loves her and would gladly divorce his wife if he could. So, she asks What if she's in jail for murder? The third woman tells him of their entire plan. He calls the cops, and she testifies in court. The two women are sentenced to twenty years in prison, and the two lovebirds take off for the Riviera and live happily ever after."

"I like it. I'm an abused character who gets a second chance." Olivia rationalized. She assumed that she was playing the lead.

Rachel raised an eyebrow, but wisely kept her mouth shut. To tell Olivia now that her character was Beatrice, sentenced to twenty years in jail for the murder of Trisha's husband, was to lose Olivia. Besides, this was perfect. Olivia was excited about the play, and she didn't even have to use Mr. McPherson's name. She could save that as an Ace up her sleeve. Because once Olivia found out she's not playing the lead, she'd walk. But hopefully by then they'd already be in rehearsals, and nobody walks out on a Mr. McPherson Production.

"That's excellent, Miss Reed. I'm looking forward to working with you." Rachel smiled. She uncrossed and crossed her legs as a man would, balancing her shoe on her knee.

Olivia noticed. "Of course, you are." She shot back snobbishly. "Just make sure my dressing room is the biggest, and of course, my name must be over the title on the marquee, and in larger letters."

There's that diva-tude. Rachel rolled her eyes as she remembered Mr. McPherson's warning. "Oh, by the way, you're invited to a New Year's Eve party at Mr. James Farrington III's penthouse condo. Cocktails are at seven."

"A New Year's Eve party? At James Farrington's?" Olivia questioned her. Olivia was sure that she had heard that name before.

Rachel nodded and confirmed, "Yes, Mr. Farrington is going to be our set designer. "

"Oh, you mean Mr. Farrington of Farrington's Interior Designs." Olivia brightened as she remembered his name.

"Yes." Rachel smiled condescendingly at her.

"He did Diana's Place," Olivia told her. She was already making plans for when she might have him come over and do her home. "Her dining room is to die for. Sevenish, you say?"

"Yes." Rachel reiterated, with a jovial smirk. *Sevenish? I wonder what time that is in Diva-land?*

"I'll be there." Olivia nodded approvingly.

"Excellent. Thank you for your time, Miss Reed." Rachel stood.

"You're quite welcome." Olivia reached over and rang for her butler. "Rogers will show you out."

Rachel bowed a gentlemanly goodbye to Miss Reed as Rogers showed up to escort her to the door. Miss Reed waved goodbye as if waving off a fly, then pondered about Ms. Rachel Washington.

"This could be interesting." Olivia rested her forefinger against her chin and thought about it with an intrigued grin.

CHAPTER 9

Rachel arrived early at James' condo. She not only helped him make room in the fridge for the food that would be coming later, but she also helped him move his furniture around to accommodate all the guests. Well, that is to say, she moved the furniture around. James just stood around, telling her where to move things and how to set up his living room for a grand party.

"No, no, no, Rachel; that should go over there. That way, the guests can have a small dance floor. And the couch should go over there, that's the best view of the windows, and the fireplace will keep their backs nice and warm."

"Will you make up your frigging mind? Or better yet, why don't you help me?" Rachel growled, and she dropped the love seat in place with an angry thud.

"Oh no dear, that's why I called you over. I need a man for manual labor."

Rachel just glared at him angrily. "I am so charging you for this."

James just raised an eyebrow and flicked a lazy wrist at her. "Darling, this is your price for holding the party here."

"Oh, you little...."

"Meow." Mr. Tabby mewed as he licked his paws. As if to say, he's right, you brute. Deal with it.

Rachel just eyed the cat with equal hatred, and then the doorbell rang.

Alex Harland, the hotshot Tennis star, had arrived. He wore a burgundy velvet dinner jacket with black satin lapels; black dress trousers were cut a little too tight, a white shirt, a black bow tie, and a cummerbund. Alex was a tennis pro and James' business partner. He had unbelievable talent with a racket in his hand, but not much else without it.

He was a cocky bastard, who used his good looks and winning record get him anything he wanted. He went to the best clubs. He went to the best parties. Even the entire advertising world wanted him to sponsor them. He was of medium height and had an athletic build. His blue eyes and winning smile made women, and some men, swoon for him.

"Alex!" James practically screamed with glee as he opened the door. "Come in, I'm so glad to see you again."

"James, how are you?" Alex asked as he handed James his coat to hang up. "You simply won't believe the year I've had. This New Year's party of yours will be the first break I've had in months." Suddenly, Alex stopped talking long enough to notice what James was wearing. James wore a double-breasted, midnight blue tuxedo, white shirt, and a black tie. "James, that suit looks fabulous on you."

"You think so?" James smiled and turned around a full 360 degrees so Alex could see everything. "Thank you. I was so hoping you would like it."

"I like it," Alex leered, moving in closer to James, like a wolf with a lamb. "You've got something cooking. So, what's the occasion?

Please tell me that there will be another job soon. The summer sun is murder."

Rachel couldn't take it anymore and could barely contain her laughter as she cleared her throat, pretending to get rid of a cough. Alex just looked at her with a questioning look.

"And you are?" Alex waved a dismissive hand in her direction.

"Oh, Alex, I'm sorry. My bad. This is Rachel Washington." James introduced her.

"Hi." Rachel smiled politely as she waved hello at Alex.

"She's going to be the one to replace Mr. Frank McPherson someday," James revealed. "And this is her party tonight."

"Oh, you're that Rachel Washington." Alex turned to face her. "I've seen some of your plays. They're funny. I like them." Alex told her as he looked her up and down. "Somehow, I thought you were a boy."

Rachel just smiled and stifled another wave of laughter that hit her. "Yeah, I get that a lot."

"Rachel is a girl. She's just manlier than most girls because her father wanted a boy." James quickly explained.

Rachel continued chuckling as she took James in her arms and kissed his cheek. "Well, being with you, one of us needs to be a boy, and it's certainly not you."

James blushed, and Alex gave him an *Is that so* look. James quickly pushed Rachel away and changed the subject by asking Alex how his flight was. He was very glad to see that Alex had come. Rachel watched dubiously as they talked, mostly about Alex and his career.

Thankfully, the doorbell rang. Rachel went and answered it. It was Mac, and he was dressed to the nines, wearing a white tie and tails. Then she noticed a royal blue sash under his coat, running over his vest. Suspended around his neck by a blue ribbon was a blue enameled cross with gold eagles between the arms of the cross. A large eight-pointed metal star was on his jacket.

"What in the hell are you wearing?" Rachel questioned him, quite perplexed.

"Like them, do you?" He greeted her warmly with a hug.

"They are nice, but don't you feel a little overdressed for a black-tie affair?" Rachel commented as she looked over his attire. "You look like an ambassador to the United Nations. What's with the sash, the cross around your neck, and what's that thing on your coat?"

"Well, my grandfather was a count from Konigshauffen." He explained as he handed her his overcoat to hang up. "When I went there two years ago for his funeral, I discovered that he named me his sole heir and successor. So, my official title is Graf Mackenzie Jefferson von Hallbach-Eunbank. The sash, the **thing** on my coat, and the cross around my neck is the Order of the Golden Eagle, an order from the Royal House to which I belong."

"Konigshauffen?" Rachel asked, wondering if such a place even existed outside of storybooks. "Never heard of it. Is it real?"

"It is a very small kingdom that borders Austria, Germany, and Switzerland."

Rachel closed the closet door, rolled her eyes, and grinned at Mac. "You're Jewish, since when do Jews become European royalty?"

Mac shrugged and offered his opinion as he followed Rachel into the living room. "Two words, The Rothschilds."

"Fair enough." She snickered.

Rachel then introduced Mackenzie to James and then to Alex. Mackenzie shook their hands and then took Rachel aside, as James and Alex continued talking to each other. Mackenzie and Rachel went to the kitchen and put all the liquor in the fridge.

"Did you know that they're both queer?" Mackenzie asked in a hushed whisper.

"How can you tell?" asked Rachel, mocking his hushed tone.

"Their handshakes are limp."

"Among other things." She snickered.

"I'm serious. They shake hands like girls. And I keep thinking I've met or seen that Alex fellow somewhere before." Mackenzie said, scratching the back of his head.

"Most likely on the post office wall." She chuckled. "And you're wrong about them both. Butch Cassidy and the Sundance Kid over there are not gay, just effeminate. They're both professional players. But what game they're playing is anybody's guess."

Then Mackenzie remembered something about theater people. The parts of women used to be played by men. *So that's it, they're actors*. "There are going to be women here tonight, right?" He wondered with dread.

"Of course, Mac. There'll be plenty of real women and probably a few witches too. Our patrons are coming tonight, and some may bring their families. Some of my actors and actresses will also be in attendance tonight." Rachel informed him. Then she got serious and looked him in the eye. "Please don't freak out, but Olivia will also be here."

"I shall contain my excitement." Mac gave a low growl. He frowned at the thought of being in Her Highness' presence once again.

"Well, contain your ***Little Mac*** while you're at it. Don't be hitting on my patron's daughters or their wives." Rachel lectured Mackenzie like a naughty schoolboy. "I need their money to put on my show, and I don't need your Shanda ruining it."

"Aw, Rachel, you are making this party a real drag. By the way, what kind of people are your backers?" Mackenzie asked as he poured himself a drink and popped a cheese cube in his mouth.

"Conservative religious types predominately, as well as your typical art patrons." Rachel slapped her palm and made a cheese cube fly into the air. She caught it in her mouth and chewed, as Mackenzie snickered hard at her.

"What is the world coming to, religious types patronizing the arts?" Mackenzie shook his head in disbelief. "The world has indeed turned upside down."

"Upside down, inside out, and backwards." Rachel tossed another cheese cube into her mouth.

"Then you had better hide them," he instructed as he tossed a thumb towards James and Alex.

"Speaking of which," Rachel approached James and Alex. "James, do you remember your promise to me?"

"Yes," James assured her, rolling his eyes at her.

"It's going to be that kind of night." Rachel narrowed her eyes on him for emphasis, then gave him a big smile.

"I understand." James nodded.

"I don't. What's going on?" Alex asked as he looked between James and Rachel.

"Rachel is producing a play for Mr. McPherson," James explained. "So, there are going to be a lot of *rich* backers here."

Alex's eyes lit up. "Oh really?"

"Yes, and we are going to leave them alone." James insisted, and he squeezed Alex's left hand hard.

"What?" Alex recoiled. "Why?"

"Because friends don't steal from friends," James said, as Alex rubbed his sore hand.

"We're not friends," Alex flung his right hand toward Rachel. "Besides, we've never robbed her."

"Alex, if any of her backers are robbed and it's traced to her, she has enough dirt on us to put us away for years."

"You mean, she has enough dirt on you." Alex distanced himself from James.

"Alex." James narrowed his eyes on him. "Promise me."

"Fine, but what about friends of friends?" Alex tested the limits of their promise.

"Friends of friends is fine," James assured Alex with a wicked grin. "It's only the ones that can be directly traced to her."

That's when the doorbell rang again. Rachel left Alex and James bickering and Mac sampling the drinks as she went and answered the door.

"Ryoko, you made it!" Rachel exclaimed happily. "Tonight, just wouldn't have been right without you here."

Mackenzie heard Rachael's excitement and wandered out of the kitchen to see what was happening. He watched Rachel as she bowed to Ryoko like a gentleman to a lady, kissed her hand, and took her coat.

"You're always such a gentleman to me," remarked Ryoko, with a sly smile.

"One of us should be, don't you think? And you're not dressed for it." Rachel snickered. "How was the ride here?"

"It was fine, all things considered. I had a very nice nap." Ryoko answered as Rachel offered her an arm and ushered her into the room.

That's when Mackenzie stepped up. He had never seen such an elegant lady. Her lacy, high-collared white dress only accentuated her high cheekbones and brought great attention to her jade-colored eyes.

Ah, the exotic orient, they really know how to grow them. Mackenzie thought with great delight at what might conspire tonight. "Good evening, ma'am. My name is Graf Mackenzie Jefferson von Hallbach-Eunbank, and it is my very great pleasure to meet you." Mackenzie said, in his most charming manner, as he kissed Ryoko's hand.

"He is also the Baron of Balderdash, the Count of Carpetbaggers, and the Earl of Great Ego." Rachel snickered as she watched Mackenzie **work his magic**.

"Do you mind? I'm working here." Mackenzie criticized her. He then gave her a **get lost, will ya** kind of look.

"Tone it down, Mac. He's not your type." Rachel warned him.

Mackenzie stopped and processed what she had just said. "He's?" Mackenzie questioned unbelievingly, and his left eye began to twitch. "But didn't you call her Ryoko?"

"His real name is Sato Ryoji. He's been my best friend and confidant since college. Sato Ryoko is his designer name, in honor of his sister, and his dresses are the stuff of legends." Rachel revealed, with an almost selfish pride.

"A man pretending to be a woman, pretending to be a fashion designer?" Mackenzie recapped as his levels of charm, wit, and lust hit new lows.

"I'm not pretending to be a fashion designer. I am one." Ryoji corrected him, and he sauntered by Mackenzie with beauty, style, and grace.

Mackenzie stared in disbelief as this beautiful woman went by him. *This is a boy?* Mackenzie pondered as he silently wept to himself. *I'm losing my touch.* "I've heard about these kinds of boys, but I never thought I'd ever see one."

"And the best one on this Earth," Rachel added. "So, treat her well and with respect."

"You mean him." Mackenzie corrected her, as he looked Ryoko over and tried to find the boy inside the dress.

Ryoji looked so damn good as a girl, Mackenzie was having a hard time keeping his little man down. Everything from her face to her swaying hips told him that this was a fine woman of breeding and class, yet this was a boy. Mackenzie could only continue to stare at Ryoko until Rachel's warning threat, and a slap against his head snapped him out of it.

"And **keep** his secret," Rachel commanded, as she balled up her fist for effect. "Or I'll break your knees."

Mackenzie just shook his head in pain and muttered. "Now that's just rude." Then Mackenzie looked up at the ceiling, shook his fist in feigned indignation, and yelled, "Hey, where da white women at?!"

Ryoko laughed at him. "He's right, Rachel. There's no one here but men, and that includes you."

"Don't worry, boys. There will be women here." Rachel assured them with great mirth.

"You're not going to wear that, are you?" Ryoko frowned with great distress as she looked over Rachel's attire.

"What? I'm legally dressed?" Rachel chuckled, looking down at her clothes.

"Legally?" Mackenzie laughed as he noticed her outfit for the first time. "Rachel, you look like a Groucho Marx reject. You should be arrested."

"Oh, come on, this is a fine white dress shirt…" Rachel claimed as she showed off her shirt.

"A shirt, no, that's a thrift store reject." Ryoko interrupted. Her fashion sense just screamed at her to fix this mess. "Whoever sold you that shirt should be brought up on charges."

Rachel grimaced, but continued, nonetheless. "A fine Black Suit..."

Ryoko sniggered lightly and interrupted again. "It's a man's suit with worn-out trousers and a jacket that just doesn't lay right because it has been pressed incorrectly too many times. Nice try, though."

Rachel feigned irritation and challenged them. "Well, I dare you to find something wrong with my black shoes."

Ryoko just pinched the bridge of her nose and shook her head. "Black combat boots are not shoes, and should never be worn outside of a combat zone."

Rachel laughed. "Well, with Mac and Olivia both here tonight, who says it won't become one. Besides, I'm wearing my lucky underwear. So, everything will be fine." Rachel laughed some more and waved them both off.

"You've got lucky underwear?" Mackenzie laughed at her, his sides almost hurting from the constant ripples of laughter making his body shake. "Don't you have to be getting lucky to have lucky underwear? Even Vulcans get laid every seven years, but you..."

"No, no, no, this'll never do," Ryoko complained. Her upset and pouting face made her look more and more beautiful. "Rachel, why must I always dress you? And why did you rent a tux? You should have just told me that you had nothing to wear."

"You were busy." Rachel laughed and brushed herself off. Forcing some of the wrinkles out of her clothes, but not nearly enough. "And I didn't want to seem like a pestering child. I can dress myself, you know."

"No, you can't." Ryoko scolded Rachel, "You're not just a playwright anymore. You're an aspiring theater magnate now. People will judge your plays by your appearance. You are the billboard that sells your plays. Come on. Let's get you into the closet and see if James or Alex has something, so

I can't get you properly dressed." Ryoko pushed Rachel towards James' bedroom.

Mackenzie laughed till there were tears in his eyes. "Why are all of my friends insane?"

CHAPTER 10

The preparations for the New Year's Eve party were finally done. The cocktails were ready to be served. The Catering Company laid out a buffet fit for three kings, and an oval dance floor had been carefully created. The waiters stood ready with cocktails and hors d'oeuvres, waiting to serve the incoming guests. By 7:10 PM, the first of the guests were beginning to arrive. This party would not only herald the beginning of a new year, but Rachel would reveal her script for the play to entreat the backers and entice the players.

The party was beginning to get into full swing as everyone from trendy art patrons to actors and actresses, to conservative religious patrons and their families began to arrive. James' penthouse soon became a sea of tuxedos and evening dresses of virtually every color and style. Mr. McPherson arrived dressed in a single-breasted black tuxedo, red vest, white shirt, and black tie. Ms. Loy was on his arm, and she looked radiant, wearing a forest-green evening dress that seemed to accentuate her bright blue eyes and long red hair. Eventually, Miss Olivia Reed made her appearance, fashionable late as usual.

When Olivia arrived at the party, she was wearing a burgundy mandarin gown and a single string of pearls around her neck. Her auburn hair was pulled into a bun on the back of her head and held together with two silver chopsticks. As she entered the party, she greeted Mr. McPherson, James, Rachel, and other theater people until she noticed Mackenzie, who was playing Hong Kong Blues on the piano. Olivia strolled over to him.

Ms. Loy noticed Olivia's measured but very determined march towards Mackenzie. "Ahoy, Captain." She informed Mr. McPherson as she gently tugged on his arm. "Stormy seas are brewing."

Both Rachel and Mr. McPherson looked over in Mackenzie's direction.

"Aye, so they are." Mr. McPherson chuckled. He knew women well and could guess what was about to happen. "Well, do ye think we should send up the storm flags and warn yonder ship?"

"Na." Rachel answered in her best imitation of a Scottish accent. "That wee little iceberg won't damage his hull. He's reinforced himself with indifference and a liberal amount of alcohol."

"Rachel, you should know her better than that." Ms. Loy commented, her eyes twinkling. "Like all icebergs, it's what you don't see that'll kill you."

"Aw, Mac can handle her. His tongue's sharper than mine." Rachel told her and handed Ms. Loy a fresh drink as a waiter glided by.

"If his tongue is sharper than yers..." Mr. McPherson laughed, and his eyes sparkled with mirth. "...then maybe we should notify the field medic of incoming casualties."

While Mr. McPherson and Ms. Loy continued to mingle with the other guests, Rachel sipped her drink and waited for the fireworks to begin. This was one performance that she didn't want to miss.

As Olivia approached him, Mackenzie made his best attempt to be civil. He grinned and said,

"Good evening, Livie. You look wonderful this evening."

Olivia looked at Mac with a smug expression, and her nose scrunched in distaste as she addressed him. "Well, if it isn't temperance's favorite poster boy."

"Ah, it's good that The Abstinence Foundation has finally found a spokeswoman." Mac retorted in a dry tone, still grinning.

Olivia looked like she had just been slapped across the face. She forced a smile, but before she could make her reply, Mackenzie cut her off.

"Look, Livie, we're through." Mackenzie's fingers continued to glide gracefully over the piano keys. "I know you hate me, but for tonight, can't you at least feign a little civility towards me?"

"You weren't too civil when you dumped me!" Olivia chastised him with a stern look.

Mackenzie's grin faded. "Livie, I'm not going to talk about it anymore. You cheated on me and in my bed. That was a betrayal that even I couldn't ignore."

Olivia was turning red with anger, but before she could reply to his jab, Mackenzie's jaw tightened, and he gave her another blast.

"Look, Livie, I'm not going to give you the satisfaction of creating a scene with you. The point that I'm making is that I don't bear you any ill will, even after everything you've done to me. Now leave me in peace. I'm not going to talk to you anymore."

Olivia's face flushed with rage, and she shrieked, "I'LL GET EVEN WITH YOU, MAC. THIS ISN'T OVER!"

Hearing Olivia's outburst, the room went silent except for Mackenzie's piano playing. Mackenzie turned his head, stared at Olivia, and chuckled at her.

"Yeah, Livie, It is. I think you've embarrassed yourself enough for one night."

Olivia's face bleached white with rage. She turned on her heels and stormed off towards the bar. As she walked away, Mac shook his head and then started to play We'll Meet Again.

With the bit of melodrama over with, the party continued, and the guests went back to drinking and talking among themselves. Music, merriment, and much banter grew to overshadow the previous scene, and all was forgotten.

The last to arrive was Rachel's childhood friend, Paul Brian Cartwright. Paul Cartwright was the second of Frank McPherson's handpicked prodigies. He had grown into a very serious man who enjoyed money and fame. He was still of medium height, medium frame, and medium nature. In fact, there was nothing memorable about him. Maybe that's why he found it so hard to get ahead. He was an average man in a world of extremes. His determined eyes of blackest hue matched his mood, and his dark brown hair covered a world of sin and pain.

He had taken to the theater because he enjoyed the irony of tragedy and horror. He had tired of the bubblegum fairy tales of his youth and wanted something more grown-up. But that was seven long years ago. Now it had become a place where he could act out all his pain and aggression and still be loved for it. He could make audiences cheer for him, laugh for him, cry for him, and even die for him, and it was all completely acceptable. He reveled in his role of demi-god, and a wicked grin spread across his face.

"Such a sea of players." He mused as he sought out his employer, Mr. McPherson.

Under Mr. McPherson's tutelage, the three of them had risen to the top of their craft, each of them becoming very successful playwrights. But now Mr. McPherson was looking for an heir to his theatrical throne. He had chosen Victoria, but then she died. So now he was grooming Rachel.

Paul tugged at his black tie and grinned. He looked sharp in his white pleated dress shirt, single-breasted black tuxedo with matching trousers, and cummerbund. He watched as Mr. McPherson personally introduced Rachel to all his wealthy backers as his new protégée.

Rachel may be my childhood friend, but that failure of an engineer doesn't have the chops for this.

Paul walked over to Mr. McPherson. He greeted Ms. Loy with a smile and a nod and then listened to Mr. McPherson praise Rachel.

"And this is mah golden girl, Miss Rachel Washington. She has a brilliant sense of irony and a sharp sense of humor. She's taken a classic and given it a modern edge. Next, she'll part the waters fur ye." Mr. McPherson praised her, with all the pride of a proud father.

"Aw, Frank, don't. I'm not a god." Rachel blushed.

"This is theater Rachel; all good writers are. And ye're a great writer." Mr. McPherson insisted, as he accepted another drink from a passing waiter.

"Rachel, Frank wouldn't waste time on the commentary if it wasn't true." Ms. Loy added, as she let go of Mr. McPherson's arm to straighten his tie a little.

Rachel smiled at the two of them and thought they were a handsome couple. But before she could think further, she heard a gentleman in front address her.

"Rachel, I'm Bishop Steven Able." He reached his hand out to her. "I'm one of Frank's oldest and dearest friends. I look forward to hearing about and maybe backing your new play." He spoke to her, smiling brightly.

Rachel turned her head towards the gentleman and shook his outstretched hand. "Thank you Bishop Able. I would appreciate any help that you can give. Mr. McPherson has often commented about your generosity."

Paul looked on with envy. His smiled remained plastered perfectly to his face, but his eyes grew dark as he remembered their shared past.

Rachel and I have been friends since fifth grade. I liked her because she was capable, full of fun and mischief. She always told me that my ideas were stupid, but she was always the first one to follow me in doing them. She was always behind me, and together we could do anything. I never worried about trouble, because she would always back me up. She even took the blame for me a couple of times. We were best friends, and I thought that would never change.

But it did change. It all changed when her father died. She then became all sad and hollow. Like her life had abandoned her, all that was left was an empty shell. That was to be expected. She was in mourning, but still. She just slammed the door in my face. She wouldn't follow me anymore. After her father died, our duo became a solo act. Shit, my parents broke up when I was eleven and you didn't see me shutting her out. In fact, she got two Christmases because of me. Luckily, mom and dad were good people...just not with each other.

And then, in her senior year of college, she found someone else, a cross-dresser named Ryoji. The first time I had met him, I thought he was a girl like everyone else. But then came that fateful day in the bathroom. Oh my god, I still can't get that image out of my head. A girl with a... Why didn't she tell me? Maybe she didn't know. No, she found someone to replace me and hid him from me. That was a betrayal of friendship that I will never forget ...or forgive.

Hell, she never even wanted to be a playwright. I suggested that she take up writing. She could always tell good stories. But now she is surpassing me, and she has never thanked me. And if that cross-dressing sycophant wasn't bad enough, she picked up one even worse. It's bad enough when one is playing at being gay, but it's even worse when one is gay.

James Farrington III, interior designer and full-time pansy. Somehow, she talked me into letting that fruitcake redecorate my room. He did a great job, but still... his choices for sexual company are unacceptable. I work my ass off and barely get noticed. She just tells a few jokes and she second in command! This is so not fair!!

Paul listened with disgust and nearly gagged as Mr. McPherson praised her for assembling her own group of actors, musicians, and designers instead of relying on his connections.

"Something wrong with ye Paul?" Mr. McPherson asked, concerned by the look on Paul's face. "You look a little sick."

Ms. Loy coughed to hide a giggle. A little sick? *No, he's a lot sick and slightly twisted too. She reflected. Just look at his plays.*

"Oh no, sir, it's just that I don't think this caviar is fresh." Paul answered with a weak smile, and he quickly picked up an hor d'oeuvres.

But he fumed even more as he listened to Rachel's pitch about her new play. He wanted to hate it; but it was so good, that even he was curious to see it. He sighed heavily, and swallowed a lump of growing depression, as everyone else gushed with excitement, and promises to do their best to make this play a hit.

And then he got very angry. *She is doing drama now, my drama. If she succeeds at this play, will Mr. McPherson even keep me around? I can't do comedy, and if I were Mr. McPherson, I wouldn't keep me around. Why keep someone around who can only do drama when you have someone who can do both drama and comedy?*

Over in the corner and observing it all was a very beautiful and serious looking woman. She had long black hair, which elegantly framed her strong angular features. She had high cheekbones, a strong jaw, and curved heart lips. She looked ethnic with her deep olive skin. She was thin almost model emaciated thin. But her real starring feature was her very black eyes. They were strangely dark and looked like they should be hiding something, but they weren't. She spoke to no one except those that dared to say hello to her.

"Great party, isn't it?" asked one of Rachel's actresses.

"Yes, it is. Quite well done." She smiled, her high cheekbones giving her the look of an aristocratic lady.

"I'm Theresa Smart. I'm playing the part of wife number three."

"Really? How interesting." She lifted her glass and toasted the young woman. "You must be very excited. I'm Renee Bailey."

"Bailey? Bailey? I've heard your name before." Ms. Smart tried to recall.

"I'm in shipping." Ms. Bailey put her glass down and gave her a small but sincere smile.

"That's right, Bailey's International Shipping." Ms. Smart cheered at her ability to remember this woman. "It's such a pleasure to meet you."

Ms. Bailey just smiled at her and with nothing more really to talk about, Theresa left to get in on a more interesting conversation. Lacking in small talk about the theater, Ms. Bailey chose to stay out of conversations. She was more interested in Paul Cartwright. She raised an eyebrow in curious contemplation as she watched him, and his reactions to all that was going on. He did not look happy about it, and unhappy people often did very interesting things.

Someone else was watching the night's activities, too, and they were making notes. Any party that Miss Olivia Reed, Queen of Broadway, attended was to be reported on and publicized. The other reporters would have given their souls to be privy to this party. But it was a very private affair. So, it was good to have friends in high places, but even better to have old school chums who were about to become stars in a Rachel Washington play.

Paul Cartwright signed heavily again, as he stood back and watched the party rage on. Then, he noticed something in Olivia as she read the script. He looked down at his copy of the script. Of course, she was angry because she wasn't playing the lead. And she wouldn't dare walk out on a Franklin McPherson production... or would she?

Olivia ordered another drink as Paul made his way over to her. He found her sitting at the bar, staring at her drink in introspection and anger. Paul took the seat beside her and ordered a glass of water. He took a slow sip and thought aloud, loud enough for her to hear.

"How dare that young upstart do that to you?"

"He's not that young?" Olivia voiced, irritated, and dryly.

"He?" Paul asked, a little puzzled. They obviously weren't talking about the same person.

"Mackenzie Jackass Eubank; the inebriate extraordinaire and worthless swine." Olivia replied exasperated.

"Oh, of course, that upstart and idiot. But no, actually I was referring to the writer of this play."

Paul said, nonchalantly, as he held his glass up to view Rachel's distorted image in it. "Rachel Washington."

"Oh, her, and what is she supposed to have done?" asked Olivia, feigning ignorance.

"To put a star such as you in a supporting role. Even if she is Mr. McPherson's favorite, she must recognize and acknowledge seasoned talent." Paul flattered her as he put his glass down on the bar. "Or maybe she doesn't, and she shouldn't be made a director at all."

Paul picked up the bottle of Chardonnay Olivia had been drinking from and refilled her glass. He smiled slyly as he watched her receive his generosity. She looked wasted or just about there. He could almost see her dark thoughts of revenge swirling around in her head.

"That's alright," Olivia said, slamming the drink down. I'll just talk to Mr. McPherson, and he'll make her change it."

"Of course he will, and he should too. He knows you're not a has-been." Paul commented, as he poured her yet another drink.

"Has been?" Olivia frowned with fear. She pulled a small mirror from her handbag and looked into it. She noticed that she did not look well. "He thinks I'm a has-been?"

While Olivia looked at her face in the mirror, Paul chuckled wickedly.

This is too easy. Too much drinking always clouds the mind and makes it easy to manipulate people. Tonight could be the biggest disaster of Rachel's life. If things go the way I planned, her career could be over, and she'd never work again. Maybe she'll even leave the city and go back to tinkering.

Olivia was still making faces in her mirror. She never noticed Paul slipping a white powder into her drink.

The ultimate aid in freeing inhibitions. Paul thought smugly, and he handed the tainted drink to Olivia. "Of course, Mr. McPherson doesn't think you're a has-been. He knows you're a great actress and should be playing the lead."

Olivia took the drink he offered her and drank it down. Paul waited for the drug to take effect.

Soon Olivia started swaying. She pinched the bridge of her nose, as if trying to clear her head. Paul smiled.

"In fact," Paul suggested, looking over his shoulder. "I think you should march right over there and tell him exactly how you feel about this slight."

"You know, you're right." Olivia agreed, and she staggered as she stood. "I'm a star and I don't have to take being treated this way."

Paul helped to steady her as he pointed her in the direction of Mr. McPherson.

"I'm going over there right now and give him a piece of my mind." Olivia declared harshly.

"That's my girl." Paul encouraged her, as he watched her head into the fray. *That's one down and more to go. He thought, as he poured and laced another drink. Okay, who's next?* That's when he spied Mac the wolf, playing the piano. Bingo. *Target acquired, and now, who shall be the lamb for the slaughter?* Paul reasoned, with devilish delight. *Ah, Miss Sarah Able, professor of European history and the only daughter of Mr.*

*McPherson's most affluent and most conservative
backer. Perfect.*

Paul sifted through the crowd like a shadow.
He seemed invisible. No one noticed him, and why
would they? He wasn't the golden child. Rachel
was. She made him sick. This should all be his:
the accolades, the offers, the respect, the fame,
and the play. Drama was **his** thing, after all.

Paul sat down at the black grand piano beside
Mackenzie. He noticed that Mackenzie didn't even
bother to make room for him there, so he just
balanced himself on the edge. He wouldn't be here
long anyway, not with what he had planned.

"Here ya' go piano man. I thought you might
be thirsty." Paul played the part of concerned fan
well. He smiled, though it was strained, and
handed him the laced drink.

"God bless you, my good man." Mackenzie
thanked Paul as his fingers stopped running across
the keys.

He picked up the drink, but the wet glass
slipped through Mackenzie's inebriated fingers.
Paul's lip twitched into a snarl as the drink spilled,

making a crystal-clear puddle on the floor. However, he quickly regained his composure as Mackenzie spoke to him.

"I'm terribly sorry, Ol' Man, it must have been the condensation on the glass." Mackenzie's fingers returned to the piano keys.

"No worries, Mac." Paul's smile was like a mask, ugly and fake. It made him look like a monstrous clown.

"I tell you what, I'll make amends my friend." Mackenzie slid over, trilling the keys with the motion, to make room for Paul.

Mackenzie called to the nearest waiter and ordered a drink. The busy server bustled to the brilliant pianist and nodded.

"Waiter, scotch on the rocks for me and get my friend here whatever he wants." Mackenzie ordered curtly.

Paul didn't want to be here anymore. He didn't want to sit next to Mackenzie anymore. He hadn't in the first place. But for his plan to work, small sacrifices could be made.

"Perrier." That was all Paul said, and the waiter disappeared.

Mackenzie grinned to himself and thought. *Hmm, we have a lot of fruit of the loom action at this party. Grapes Galore is sitting next to me, Cherry and Banana are bickering over in the corner, and an Apple of a boy-girl sitting with the ritzy artists, probably taking about shoes.*

"Do you like Frank Sinatra?" Mackenzie asked, as he pulled a melancholy voice from the piano. It was like his very soul was pulling the music from the beautiful instrument.

"Who doesn't?" Paul shrugged, having absolutely no idea who Frank Sinatra was.

"Quite right." Mackenzie nodded, as he started to play Witchcraft. The music was dazzling and consuming to the pianist.

"Say Mac, have you noticed that Nubian goddess Sarah Able over there?" Paul asked, as he looked in her direction.

Mackenzie looked up from his playing and saw Dr. Sarah Rebecca Able, PhD, the only daughter of Bishop Dr. Steven Able and his wife Mary. He saw her, and it was oddly like he was seeing a woman for the first time.

Dr. Sarah Rebecca Able was a tall, pear-shaped woman. She wore her dark plum gown like a glove. It fell off her shoulder to grip her pert, round breast and just wide enough hips. It was perfect against her cinnamon-colored skin as it swept the floor. Her face looked like it should have been sculpted. Her features were sharp and regal. She was a masterpiece of symmetry and shape. Her large brown eyes seemed to be faceted like gemstones.

Whoa, such a vision of beauty; even Venus would envy. Mackenzie thought to himself. *Heaven must have lost one of its angels this evening. Either that, or Satan is tempting me into hell.*

"A woman like that isn't noticed, she's worshiped." The lust glazed Mackenzie eyes and drew his talented hands from the keys again.

"Want to meet her?" Paul asked pointedly. "I'm sure you need a break anyway. Why not take fifteen?"

"Fifteen? Hell, a woman like that deserves an hour at least...maybe more...hopefully all night." Mackenzie chuckled, his mind softened by alcohol and the haze of music. He stood up with a purpose.

Paul smiled. "Right this way, Mr. Eubank." Mackenzie was far too interested in Sarah to notice the madness in Paul's grin, or the aura of wrong that seemed to roll off him.

"Whoa friend, why don't you bring her over here?" Mackenzie dropped back down on his piano bench and stared at Sarah. "I am always sexier behind the keys."

"Well, I thought you would want a break?" Paul's irritation made his mask crack a fraction. The comment had come out a hiss and it was enough to make even Mackenzie, inebriated and horny as he was, suspicious.

"I tend to work better around a piano, that's all I am trying to say."

Mackenzie smiled amiably. He trilled on the keys again and decided he was cutting himself off for the night. The alcohol was making him paranoid. In truth, it wasn't. Paul didn't like this; he hated it, but decided to play the game Mac's way. After all, it really didn't matter who came to whom so long as he could get the two together and let Mac's nature take its course.

"Sure, Mac. She can admire your…fingering, right?" Paul's mask was snapped firmly back in place.

"I'm better at blowing…my sax." Mackenzie gave him a lopsided bedroom grin.

With that drool comment, Paul left Mackenzie and went to see Miss Sarah Able. On the way, he overheard an argument brewing as he passed by James and Alex, but he would get to them later. For now, he walked over to Sarah and introduced himself to her.

"Hello, Dr. Able. My name is Paul. Paul Cartwright."

"Oh, hello." She smiled politely. She was going to say it was nice to meet you; after all, she had been saying it all evening. But somehow, this person struck her wrong. Sarah let her eyes rove over Paul's skinny frame and barely hid her grimace. "Are you enjoying the party?"

"Yes," Paul lied, quite artfully. "Yes, I am. How do you like our pianist this evening? I'm told he's quite good, but I can't see the talent. What do you think?"

"It's not bad," Sarah told him. "But I haven't been listening to the music."

Paul grinned at her remark and pointed in the direction of the piano.

"Well, do you see the overdressed guy over there playing the piano?"

Sarah looked at him quizzically. Her pretty face was remade into a question mark, her perfect features melding into confusion.

What is he wearing? Is that a royal crest? Sarah looked back at Paul. "Yes, I do." She ran her delicate and extremely valuable surgeon-like hands through her hair, correcting a wayward strand. "Why?"

Paul decided on a quick approach, no reason to let people think that he was up to something. "Well, the piano player mentioned that he really admires you. And he's intolerably shy, so I would like to introduce you to him. You know, just to say hello." Paul's mask fit tighter into place, as he plastered on another smile. "Would you mind sparing a minute or two?"

Sarah didn't answer him right away. She stood and listened to the music being played. It was as if the music would decide her answer. The piano player wasn't half bad. Actually, he was pretty good.

Well, it couldn't hurt just to meet him. Sarah thought. "Alright," Sarah agreed. She gave Paul a slight smile. "Lead the way."

"Great."

Mackenzie had switched tunes and was now playing a Fats Waller tune, "Ain't Misbehavin'." When they got to the piano, Paul introduced Sarah to Mackenzie. Sarah watched as Mackenzie swayed with the music, his eyes closed. She could almost hear the piano sing, like it had a voice. Sarah smiled. Mackenzie was amazing.

"Hey Mac, I would like to introduce you to Miss Sarah Abel, PhD." Paul introduced Sarah to him.

He stepped aside and gently guided Sarah closer to Mackenzie.

"It is always a pleasure to meet such a lovely lady." Mackenzie stopped playing and focused all his attention on the goddess before him.

"Dr. Able, this is Mr. Mackenzie Eubank." Paul continued.

Mackenzie stood up, took Sarah's hand, and bowed, as he clicked his heels in greeting. "Good evening, Dr. Abel, I'm Graf Mackenzie Jefferson von Hallbach-Eunbank at your service."

"A Count, eh, I'm delighted." Sarah flushed at the old 1930s charm and gave him a light curtsy.

"You know German titles?" Mackenzie asked. His lecherous gaze lightened to one of mild surprise and infinite respect. It wasn't a stretch to say he was pleasantly surprised.

Sarah smiled. It glittered, and notes in forte ran through Mackenzie's head.

"I teach European Art History at the University."

"In that case, Doctor, please." Mac gestured to the piano bench. "I would be honored to have you join me."

Sarah did so, and the two began to converse.

Paul slowly slithered back into the crowd. He knew his mission was accomplished. Mackenzie moved closer to Sarah, drawing her in with the soul of a musical genius, but with the intent of a horny frat boy. He played, and they swayed together, entranced by the sound. His arm slid around her to the point where she was now sitting in his lap, as he made the piano sing and weep.

Paul grinned, the insanity and bitterness flashing through his eyes and into his smile. He watched for progress from time to time as he prepared another drink. Then he leaned against a wall, invisible and unheard. But they'd hear him all right. This was his masterpiece. This was his piece of art. He was performing in a living play. Manipulating his cast to just the conclusion he wanted...and Paul was a master of morbid tragedy.

Mackenzie whispered in Sarah's ear. She would laugh, and then she would do the same to Mac, and then he would laugh. They were so happy, entertained by art and music... lust and lullabies.

Having successfully left the lamb with the lion, Paul returned his attentions to **Othello**. Paul watched them for a bit, looking for an opening and building dramatic tension before he made his entrance. His opportunity came when Alex got up to get James a drink. Paul took Alex's position on the blue love seat and warmly greeted James.

"Here you go, Mr. Farrington. A good drink from a loyal friend, not like some people." He said as he handed James the drink.

James took the drink and sipped it. It was good, spicy with a nice kick? Was it bourbon?

"Some people?" James inquired curiously.

"Yeah, some people. You know, people like fair-weather friends...or lovers." Paul said it so innocently as he reclined and placed an arm on the armrest. He was playing a different part. He was becoming who he needed to be for this scene.

He was the antagonist and needed the trust of the supporting character. "Many people are only here for what you can give them."

"Fair weather lovers?" James asked, taking another sip of Paul's tainted drink. "Oh, we're not…"

"So, Rachel didn't tell you about Alex's affair last summer?" Paul feigned surprise; he looked down and cleared his throat, injecting guilt into his next lines. "I'm sorry. I would never have said anything if I had known you weren't aware. But since I told you, you should know the whole story."

"Alex had an affair last summer?" James repeated it like a stunned parrot. "With whom?"

"It was during the British Open, remember? The British tabloids had a field day with it. That's why I assumed you had to know."

"Oh, that was just a misunderstanding," James said. He gave a feminine flick of his wrist to brush away the bad thoughts. "Alex told me that nothing happened."

"Nothing happened?" Paul scowled and patted James' shoulder comfortingly. He leaned forward to face James. "He lied. It was more like a good luck breakfast after a night of very good luck. I can't believe Rachel didn't tell you. I guess she must be better friends with Olivia than she is with you."

"Olivia?! It was Olivia?!" James' high-pitched shriek drew attention from the other guests. He instantly shut his mouth and grated his teeth, before downing the rest of his drink in one big gulp. "Alex told me that...He promised me that he wouldn't fleece any of Rachel's friends." James growled.

"Fleecing?" Paul snickered. "Is that what they're calling it now? Well, then he sheered her real good. But still, he was with someone other than you, wasn't he?" Paul pondered aloud so James could hear him. "Are you sure he's not bi-sexual? I mean look how he holds his tennis racket."

"How does that even matter?" James was seething, impressionable, and under Paul's control. *He promised me that he would never steal from Rachel's friends, and in return, Rachel has kept our secret. I wonder how many of Rachel's friends he's been stealing from behind our backs. James' attention returned to the present only when Paul addressed him again.*

"He uses both hands. I can't believe you've never noticed. He's ambidextrous. Maybe you don't know him as well as you think. Two hands can easily become two-faced, don't you think?"

Paul got up and left, passing by Alex, who was carrying a nice martini. Alex returned to his seat with James' fresh drink. Paul smiled as he noticed James didn't thank Alex for bringing him another drink. This was all falling apart quite nicely.

"What's wrong, James? You seem put out." Alex inquired as he sat back and crossed his legs. Took a sip of his drink and surveyed the room. "Are you sure we can't just scope out...?"

"Tell me what happened last summer in Britain," James asked meaningfully. "No lies this time! What happened during the British Open?"

"Oh, not this again." Alex groaned, and his shoulders slumped. He pinched the bridge of his nose, and then he turned to face James. He smiled at him warmly and tried to calm him down. "You're being paranoid, James. I told you what happened last summer."

"I have it on good authority that it was more than that!" James' voice was acid and ate away at Alex's calm. "Was it more?"

"Now what's that witch Olivia been telling everybody!?" Alex glared at his drink and even considered throwing it, but it wouldn't do to ruin James' house. He stayed here most of the time. "I tell you she's obsessed with me! She thinks we're in love and that she's the greatest thing in my life since the invention of tennis balls! Especially, since that drunk ass at the piano dumped her!"

"Alex, don't you trust me with the truth? You know I hate liars more than Mr. Tabby hates cheap tuna." James' heart ached at the perceived betrayal. *Why is Alex lying to my face*? "You promised me that we'd never pinch from friends."

"First, don't you trust me at all?! If I say nothing happened, then nothing happened! Second, Ms. Reed is not one of Rachel's friends. She was only dating that Mackenzie guy."

Their raised voices drew odd stares from some of the guests, but only momentarily, as they judged it nothing more than a distraction. After all, this was only the second time that raised voices had been heard.

"It's just that you've been so distant lately," James complained as he shook his head, highly displeased with Alex's reckless behavior. "I have to believe it's because you've found another partner. I've noticed that you hold your racket with both hands. Tell me...are you...?"

"Distant?! I've been playing tennis! I played in the Barclays ATP World Tour, the BND Paribas Masters, and the Fed Cup Final. Not to mention, I've got to start practicing for the three major open tournaments I've got next year; the U.S., British and French. I have two commercials to do and a public appearance to make at the end of the month!" Alex gripped James, pushing him back to stare right into his eyes. "I'm not distant, I'm busy. I finally get a break during the winter, and I choose to spend New Year's with you, and this is how I'm treated?"

"I'm sorry, Alex. It's just..." James began to feel a little sheepish for being so petty.

"Look, James, be fair. Do I bother you when you've got showrooms, private homes, and play sets to design? Do I say you're being distant when you run yourself ragged finding paint colors, fabrics, and textures?" Alex interrupted his cohort, who was growing more flustered. "I think you could at least be a little bit more understanding. Besides that, what about you and Rachel? You two looked awfully cozy together this afternoon. I know she's a girl, but she's one butch tomboy, and I know you admire dominate men." Alex raised an eyebrow at James.

"Rachel?" gasped James, as he looked to Rachel, who was chatting up her potential patrons. He watched her laugh as one of them must have told a good story. "I've known her for years, but there is nothing there. We're just friends and we'll never be anything more than that. She's the daughter of a Marine MP. She's too honest to be one of us."

"Oh really? You two looked quite friendly to me this afternoon. What was she doing in your house all day anyway?" Alex snapped and he leaned back to give James tit for tat. "You're planning something, I know it. Are you trying to cut me out or cut me loose?"

"Alex, you know I would never! She was moving furniture around for me, and that is all!" James faced Alex.

"Then why don't you believe me?!" Alex asked, as he sprang forward like a 'jack in the box'. "If I say nothing happened, then nothing happened."

"It's just that we must be careful," James complained. For all his sophistication and style, he was concerned about his partner. I can't help thinking about what you're doing, where you might be, and who you spend time with. Maybe Rachel is right. Perhaps we should go legit."

"Yeah, well, how do you think I felt when you went off to Spain without me?" charged Alex, as he fell back into his side of the couch. This fight was draining him. He just wanted to sleep now. "I swear if it weren't for your insistence on having a legit front, I could live happily on a beach somewhere with my ill-gotten goods. And what do you mean that **she** wants us to go straight?"

"Rachel knows we make just as much money legally as we do from larceny. She thinks that we should retire and live a good life." James whispered to his partner.

Alex narrowed his eyes on James. "I live by my own rules. Not by hers. If you want out of the gang, then leave. I'm tired of living by your rules anyway. From now on, I will live, love, and pilfer who I want and when I want."

"Speaking of which, I got a strange phone call while I was in Spain. A woman was looking for you. She said you took something from her. Just what were you doing while I was gone?" accused James, crossing his arms and waiting for an answer.

That did it; now Alex was mad. "Oh, for crying out loud, James!" Alex ranted as he threw his arms into the air at the absurdity of this. "I'm an international tennis star! I'm freaking rich! Women are always trying to marry me or claim that I'm the father of their children. It should be on the list of job requirements. They just want money! And I took nothing from her financially or sexually!"

All the faces in the room looked towards them, and both men sat stunned and flailing for some excuse as they coughed and cleared their throats. Thankfully, everyone seemed to just return to their own business as James and Alex toned down their argument.

"Heh, heh, heh, this is better than watching soaps," Paul remarked with an amused chuckle. "And now for teacher's pet." His malicious intent made his lope more of a jog, and he laced one last drink.

As Paul approached, Mr. McPherson told Rachel how proud he was of her. Paul plastered on a smile and pretended to be cheerful. As Paul approached, Ms. Loy's smile dropped. She turned and whispered in Mr. McPherson's ear.

"Frank, here comes your pet creep." Ms. Loy pressed herself to Mr. McPherson and bit his ear gently.

She didn't trust that man and didn't want him to know she had warned Frank about him. Mr. McPherson shot her a disapproving look, but it was lost on her as she nibbled his ear.

"Good evening, Paul. Ye look very trim this evening." Mr. McPherson greeted him.

"Thank you, sir." Paul smiled as he straightened his expensive jacket, hoping they would notice. I just thought I would look my best for Rachel's big day."

Mr. McPherson raised his shoulder an inch. Ms. Loy took the hint and released Mr. McPherson's ear. "I'm sorry, Paul. I was preoccupied. I'm glad you could make it." She smiled politely.

It was natural. It was normal, and it irritated the hell out of Paul. He didn't show it, though. He clamped down on his urge to scream whore at Ms. Loy and just smiled wider.

"Thanks, Ms. Loy. Your dress is stunningly beautiful, just like you are. Frank is a lucky man."

"Keep that up and Frank will think yer ag bualadh on his girl," Rachel chuckled, imitating an Irish accent. "He's Scottish, he'll clobber you with a Shillelagh."

Paul looked at Rachel and gave her an obviously feigned grin. "He's Scottish, Rachel. That is an Irish accent, and don't you ever wear girl's clothes? Ms. Loy here looks like a lady." Paul gritted his teeth, jealous that her suit was better than his. "Why not borrow some of Rollie's clothes? Oh, wait; you don't fit Ryoko's clothes, do you?"

It was said like an insult and packed the bite of a cobra. Rachel growled at Paul. *Was she a lady? Yes. Was she surrounded by potential patrons in a public place? Yes. Would any of that stop Rachel from slugging Paul and dropping his skinny ass into a submission pin? Hell no!*

"Don't insult my friends; that's Miss Sato to you." Rachel's eyes grew dark. She clenched her right fist at her side and seemed much taller than her five feet six inches.

"Now, now, kids. Let's nae rammy." Mr. McPherson scolded them, as he stood between his two pissed protégés like a fight referee. He was all six feet plus and Scottish power. Rachel backed down, and so did Paul. He had to play the submissive weakling for his plan to work.

"He's right. Tonight is a night for cheer and congratulations." Paul said as he handed Rachel her **poison apple** martini drink. She was Snow White. She was the fairest of them all, and now she would fall to her fate. "To Rachel, break a leg, girl."

"Well said, Paul. Tae Rachel, break a leg mah lassie." Mr. McPherson praised her as he pulled Ms. Loy to him and clinked his snifter to her matching one.

Paul looked through the bottom of his glass as he drained his drink. He wanted to see *little snow white* fall into his trap. He wanted to see the very second she fell to the ground and never wake up again.

Mr. McPherson spoke again when he finished his drink.

"Don't worry, Paul; I have a play in mind fur ye too." Mr. McPherson clapped Paul on the shoulder and nodded. "Ye'll git yer chance to lead and very soon too. I just need tae obtain the rights."

"No, thank you, sir. I'm just glad to be your playwright. Give me too much power and you might corrupt me." Paul chuckled with very controlled laughter.

Paul's voice was gritty and felt like sandpaper to Ms. Loy's ears. She shuddered slightly as he laughed.

"Don't worry, Paul. No matter how big I get, I know who my friends are," Rachel told him. She grinned, her previous anger fading away in a giddy, foggy cloud of alcohol and drugs.

"Do you now?" Paul asked, no longer smiling as he eyed her.

"Frank, Amanda!" Mary, Bishop Able's wife, called to them over the din of the happy party. "Over here, please, you must see this."

"Excuse us, you two." Mr. McPherson nodded at them in passing as he and Ms. Loy left to join Mrs. Able.

Paul watched them leave and then turned his attention back to Rachel. But Rachel's gaze was preoccupied. Paul followed her gaze and saw Ryoko. Ryoko was standing near the window and looking out into the night. *I hate the fact that such a beautiful woman is really a boy. I also hated that Rachel had someone to call her own, and I don't. If Ryoko had been a real girl, I would have asked her out, and then Ryoko would have been on my arm. But no, Ryoko is a boy, and he is with Rachel. Rachel had it all: a play, a partner, and soon she would have Frank's empire. And what I do have...nothing. But I am going to change that.*

"Ryoko's a pretty boy," Paul mentioned nonchalantly.

"Yes, 'course he is." Rachel's words slurred as they left her mouth, but her eyes never left Ryoko's form. She giggled as she watched Ryoko twirl her hair absently around a delicate finger. He really was a lady. It was so strange, and yet...so cute. "He's pretty inside an' out. 'Sides you, he's my oldest and dearest friend."

"We've been friends since elementary school." Paul reminded her. He could barely hide the hurt in his voice. "You didn't meet him until our senior year in college. So, how did you meet him anyway?"

"We met in a graveyard." Rachel mused, recalling the first time she had met her girl-friend.

"When? At midnight?" Paul scoffed at her, only half caring to hear the tale.

Rachel looked at Paul and laughed. It was a bubbly, enchanted sound.

"No, it was late one rainy afternoon. At the Cantbee Memorial Cemetery, twelve years ago. It was exactly one week after my father died. I went to my father's grave to visit him, and I saw this beautiful girl all dressed in black, standing in front of three graves...all alone. I usually don't butt into other's people's personal business; but that day something told me to go and talk to her." Rachel leaned against the doorframe behind her. She was getting dizzy. *How much did I drink?* She wondered, as she crossed her arms and smiled lazily at Ryoko. The sight of him just made her feel good all over.

"You were saying, Rachel?" The sharp, unnoticed edge to Paul's voice brought her back.

"Right, sorry. I cleared my throat as I approached. I didn't want to scare her. So, I said the only thing that I could think of...."

Rachel recalled the scene in her mind's eye as if it had just happened yesterday. It was a dark and grey day full of sorrow and remorse, made even worse by the downpour of rain. Only two people had dared to brave the weather that day.

**

"I'm sorry for your loss," Rachel said as she stood beside the weeping figure.

The girl just stood there, protected from the rain by her big black mushroom-like umbrella, but not from the unbelievable pain and grief in her heart. She seemed like a statue, so stiff and strained, like she would crack if she moved. She didn't even look at Rachel as she spoke.

"And I am sorry for yours."

Not knowing what else to say, Rachel just stood beside her. She just kept her company in her sorrow. *Hey, misery loves company, and this girl really looks miserable.* Rachel looked down at the graves. This girl had lost her mother, her father, and her brother.

"Ryoji, your brother," Rachel began, reading the name on the grave.

"We both died very young," She said, her eyes red from crying. "We were ten years old when that school bus crashed. I survived, but she didn't. But my parents had been told that I died and that she had survived."

"So that's why you said that you both died that day. I'm sorry." Rachel said, most sincerely. "I know what it's like when your parents don't want you. My parents wanted a boy but got me instead."

The girl nodded in agreement. "I can feel your pain. I've been there and I'm still there."

Rachel didn't know this person or her brother, yet her heart was breaking. Rachel didn't bother to hide her tears as they fell. She didn't care that she was getting soaked in the rain. She didn't care that under that giant black mushroom umbrella and black dress was a stranger. She just wanted to help the person hurt less. Her eyes were dry, and she still stood, still like a rigid stone, so Rachel cried for her. For her sister...and her mother and father.

"And your parents, both in the same week," Rachel mentioned as she read their gravestones.

"One just couldn't live without the other. Father went first, and mother followed, " the girl explained, with distress in her heart but no tears left to cry.

"Are you alone now?" Rachel asked softly.

"Yes." The girl confirmed.

"So am I." Rachel sighed heavily.

That's when the girl turned and faced Rachel. The big black umbrella now covered them both. With the rain no longer blinding her, Rachel was captivated by her new friend's green eyes. They were greener than any field of grass she had ever seen. The girl placed a gentle hand over Rachel's heart and looked her in the eyes.

"You have a good and kind heart," she said, with a small smile. This expression made her beautiful and real. It removed the stone stiffness from her body and seemed to brighten the entire day. "Never lose it, and you will live a good and happy life."

Then Rachel noticed something odd about her newfound friend. "You're a boy," pronounced Rachel, very bluntly.

The girl's face fell, and she pulled away from Rachel. The boy dressed as a girl turned and tried to run away, but Rachel reached out and grabbed him by his arm. Rachel pulled him to her and looked deep into his green eyes.

"So that's what you meant when you said that she died. It confused me for a bit, but you're pretending to be your sister. You're Ryoji. Only a truly noble son would sacrifice so much for his parents' happiness."

The boy stopped trying to pull away from her. He just stared at her in disbelief. He was waiting to be called a freak...a fag...a drag queen...anything but noble. He blinked and dropped his umbrella as his arms went slack. Rachel smiled, and she bowed to him right there in the rain. How else was a gentleman supposed to greet a noble lady?

"My name is Rachel Isabella Washington, and it would be my great honor if you would join me for dinner."

At first, he said nothing. He just stared at her in disbelief. Who was this girl who bowed before him? Rachel stood and waited for his answer. Then she saw him smile. He curtsied before her, low and grand.

"My name is Sato Ryoji, and I would be delighted to have dinner with you."

**

Paul shook his head and snorted in disgust. The sound ended Rachel's story like ice water in your morning shower. She just smirked at him and then returned her gaze to Ryoji.

"That's the most twisted tale of Romeo and Juliet I've ever heard." Paul scoffed, more jealous than sympathetic.

"Ha, ha, you're right. His parents wanted a girl, and my parents wanted a boy. What are the cosmic odds that two confused nutjobs would end up finding each other in this world?" Rachel let her head lean against the wall as she tried to think through the fogginess. "Must be something like a million to one, right?"

"Ryoko looks lonely," Paul said flatly.

Rachel looked at Ryoko. He was lovely in that pure white dress, looking out the window at the black night sky—the complete opposite of the day they met. Paul noticed Rachel's eyes drooped, like she was half asleep. Her soft smile betrayed her thoughts.

"I think you should ask him to dance, don't you?" Paul whispered. His suggestion sounded friendly and oddly sweet, but the sweetness hid a poison, like cyanide's almond taste.

"Yes, I do." Rachel nodded, her head bobbing loosely with an inebriated smile.

Mackenzie had long since been too preoccupied with Sarah in his lap to keep playing. So, Rachel pulled a CD from James' collection and put it into the stereo. Black Coffee by Crystal Theory began to play.

"I'm feeling mighty lonesome. I haven't slept a wink. I walk the floor, watch the door, and in between I drink...black coffee."

"Ryoko," Rachel called as she walked up to the pretty boy dressed in white.

Ryoko turned around and faced Rachel. She smiled at her, but was puzzled by her actions.

God, he is a beautiful boy. Rachel bowed to him like a gentleman. With a drunken grin and her hand held out like a Victorian suitor, she looked adorable. "May I have the honor of this dance?" she asked him gallantly.

"Are you sure that's wise?" Ryoko questioned her with a perplexed look.

"Why not? You're dressed as a girl, and I'm dressed in one of Alex's suits. We'll just be another couple dancing." Rachel assured her with a warm grin.

"But there's a big difference between us, Rachel." Ryoko reminded her yet again, concern for her friend coloring her face. "People ***think*** I'm a girl, but they ***know*** you're a girl."

"I do not care what people think. I only wish to dance with the man I love." Rachel told him truthfully and offered Ryoko her hand again with a coy grin. "Dance with me...Ryoji."

"Love?" Funny how one four-letter word could make your world brighter than all the suns in the universe. "You're in love with me?" A stunned Ryoji let Rachel lead him out onto the dance floor.

Rachel took Ryoko in her arms and led the dance. Ryoji followed, just like they always did. It was a natural flow for them. They breathed together, their bodies so in sync that they seemed to be one person. Their heartbeats slowed, and Ryoji wondered if he would ever really need oxygen again. Ryoji was so content in her arms as he followed Rachel's strong lead.

They were perfect in every step. Every twirl of the intricate dance they created was as natural as the breathing Ryoji had given up. Ryoji's long black hair fluttered, and his eyes slipped closed. There was no need to see when you knew where you were going. No need to breathe when you are in heaven. The small gap between them got smaller as they swayed. Soon, they were pressed together like the perfect fit they were. They just clicked.

Ryoji looked down at Rachel as they danced. It was strange that he was taller, and yet it always felt like he was looking up at her. He always followed her. He never once wanted to lead. She had never once laughed at him for wearing women's clothes. And a long time ago, she had even called him a noble son.

She is the first person I have ever met in my miserable life who thinks like that. Most people laugh at me, try to beat me up, or peek under my dresses. Most condemned my actions, never once trying to see my side of the story, but not her.

She always treats me with dignity and respect. She always defends me when others taunt me. She even beat up a man twice as big as her, because he had dared to put his hands on me.

Rachel and I are more than friends. We are family. In fact, we are the only family that each of us has ever relied on. Suddenly, he noticed something else: the song they were dancing to.

"Man is born to go a-loving. A Woman's born to weep and fret. Stay at home and tend her oven. And drown her past regrets in coffee and cigarettes." The singer on the record continued to sing.

"It's our song!" Ryoji did more than smile. He beamed. It was like every strand of his original handmade white dress was glittering. "That's the song that was playing the night we first met. The very first time you took me to dinner."

"The rain and that song just seemed to fit. Even now, this song's lyrics always echo in the back of my mind." Rachel let the lilting tune guide her feet.

"That's because its words are true." Ryoji sighed, sinking deeper into Rachel's arms. "We are born to weep and fret."

Rachel stopped dancing and looked lovingly at Ryoji. "Fret not. I swear never to go a-loving anyone but you." Then she chuckled at him. "Besides, you don't smoke."

That's when Rachel kissed Ryoji. At first, Ryoji was shocked and wanted to pull away, but Rachel's kiss was so deep, passionate, and full of longing that he closed his eyes and enjoyed his first real kiss. When he stopped trying to pull away, Rachel pulled him closer and wrapped her arms around his waist, and instinctively, Ryoji's arms wrapped around her neck.

"Got you!" Paul's wicked Cheshire smile spread as he slowly made his way over to Bishop Steven Able. "Bishop Able."

Bishop Steven Nicholas Able, PhD, was a tall, stout man. He was proud of his traditional and conservative beliefs. His sharp black eyes were all-knowing and well-aged. His neatly groomed dark brown hair and his prim circular glasses gave him the air of a respectable **hanging** judge.

And although this tall African American male looked proud and unapproachable, he had an understanding heart and a keen sense of humor. And though most people didn't know it, Bishop

Able had met his wife at one of Mr. McPherson's plays. That it was Bishop Able's wife, Mary who had introduced him to Mr. Franklin McPherson. Now, as unlikely as these two men may be, they both shared the same dream: a vision to lead people down the path of light through entertainment.

"Yes, Paul. What is it?" Bishop Able gave Paul his full attention.

"Bishop, you are a Baptist, correct?" Paul began.

"Yes, I'm a proud man of faith," the Bishop replied, gently straightening his tie. "Are you?"

"Yes, sir, indeed. I was raised in my grandmama's church." Paul mimicked Bishop Able's stance to better ingratiate himself with the good bishop. "She was a great prayer warrior, she was."

"That's good. Far too few of the young people care about their souls these days. They need someone to guide them in faith and keep them on the straight and narrow path. But like they say, there is no rest for the wicked, and sin is all around us." Bishop Able jested.

"Indeed, how right you are, Bishop. Sin is all around us, even at this very party." Paul informed him rather slyly, as he prepared to guide the good bishop's attention.

"What? This seems like a very respectable affair. Most people aren't even being loud," Bishop said, glancing at James and Alex. "They were a bit noisy earlier, though, must have gotten caught up in their conversation."

"Well, I don't condone homosexuality and fornication." Paul gave his best performance of being offended. "Does the Baptist church?"

"No, we do not. We don't judge people who live that life, but it is most certainly not approved of in our doctrine." The Bishop began to frown.

Hypocrite! That single word ran through Paul's mind as a shout. He hated religion himself. It stifled people and made them sheep. It forced them to stomp down natural urges. It was full of liars wanting to make themselves feel better. *You and your church say you don't condone fornication, but I bet you were banging your wife before you were married! Not to mention your daughter is probably screaming Mac's name in soprano right now.* Paul took a breath and placed a somber, relieved expression. "I'm glad you agree that sin should be pointed out and avoided." Paul gave him a serious look.

"Yes, it is best to avoid temptation." The bishop added, his righteous attitude causing his New Year's cheer to wane. "Don't give an alcoholic wine for Christmas, you know."

"Then I humbly suggest that you wash your hands of this production. It is most certainly against your principles." Paul informed him. Then he directed Bishop Able's attention around the room. "If you look over there, you'll see Alex and James, who were gay lovers until James found out that Alex had an affair last summer with Miss Olivia Reed. That's why they were yelling at each other.

Over at the piano, you'll notice the lack of our court musician, who seems to have disappeared to sink his lecherous claws into someone's daughter.

And there, on the dance floor, in full view of everyone, is Rachel, our golden child, kissing her female fashion designer. Like you said, Sin is all around us, my fellow follower of God. I know Rachel loves her dress designs, but that's going a little too far, don't you think?" Paul asked, his face as placid as his grin.

The change in the Bishop's expression was noticeable. While moments before he looked jovial and agreeable, now he looked livid and zealous. He was a pawn, and Paul, the ultimate stage director, led him right into his next scene. It would be a glorious upbeat number with yelling and a pleasant crescendo of indignation.

"God, almighty! I thought Rachel was a decent girl. She's a lesbian? And she invited such a lecherous demon here to prey on innocent women. I cannot support that!" The Bishop barely refraining from yelling. "That's...that's...just..."

"Ludicrous...sick, wrong, and unnatural." Paul shifted his face like an expert actor into a mask of upset and major disgust. He flowed with the bishop's anger and insult. He poured oil on a raging fire, setting up for the explosion. "Not to mention...ungodly. I, myself, have nothing to do with this... I'm only here for my boss. Which I hear, he and his lady friend make the walls shake at the office."

Mr. McPherson, Ms. Loy, and Mrs. Able wandered over to join them, smiles of fun still placed on their faces. But Mrs. Able noticed that her husband was upset. It was evident in the tension of his shoulders, the tight set of his jaw, and the intense fire in his eyes.

"Steven, dear, what's wrong? You look positively livid." Mary asked her husband.

"Mary, get your coat. We're leaving! I refuse to have any part with this monstrosity!!" Bishop Able's voice carried over the hushed, intimate party and drew many faces to him, Mr. McPherson, and his wife.

Paul decided that now would be a good time to make himself scarce. He had already lit the fire and poured the gas; now, he needed to get to a safe distance, out of range of the ticking time bomb.

"Why, Steven? What on earth has gotten into ye? Ye have always been a loyal supporter of mine. This has the potential tae be a great work." Mr. McPherson stepped back, insulted that his supporter, better yet, his friend would call him a monstrosity.

"Frank, I have backed many of your productions for several years now. Many members of my congregation have also backed your plays. We love how your art portrays life. However, I have to draw the line when the lives of your associates start portraying a degenerate, slothful, and disgraceful art form." Bishop Able's yelling made a hush fall over the gawking patrons of the party. "Especially when your protégé is behaving in shall we say a very questionable manner. And I have heard that you and your **_lady friend_** are rather shameless yourselves. I can't back something that goes against the very basics of my beliefs!!"

Mr. McPherson's jaw dropped, and Ms. Loy felt his grip tighten on her shoulder. She let herself be pulled tighter against him, as he glared at the bishop.

"Now, see here, Dr. Able. I respect yer beliefs and would never ask ye tae back something that conflicted with them. But I will nae stand here and have ye insult mah employees and me. Ye claim tae be a man of God, yet ye sit here and judge us on a RUMOR!? I never figured ye one fur gossip!"

Bishop's eyes widened at the verbal slap. He cleared his throat and tugged his wife's arm roughly before he spat at Mr. McPherson. "Frank, you just lost a patron and a friend. I am pulling any donation you got from my congregation and me. Tell that to your lesbian playwright and your gay set designer!!"

Paul was safely back at the bar and on the verge of applause as he leaned against it. A delightfully wicked grin spread across his face as he sipped his drink and pretended to be disinterested in the proceedings.

Superb! My casting was impressive, and it was filled with passion, Zeal, and perfection. The scene ends with the Bishop storming off with his wife. Bishop Able, you have done magnificently.

"Lesbian?" Both Mr. McPherson and Ms. Loy muttered in disbelief, as they scanned the room looking for Rachel.

That was when they saw Rachel and Ryoko in a lover's embrace right on the dance floor. What the hell had happened while they were mingling? Ms. Loy also saw Alex and James, who were one minute bickering like **husband and wife** and the next minute not speaking at all. Mr. McPherson wondered and worried about where Mackenzie was. God only knew where Mackenzie was.

"Oh no, where's Mac?" Mr. McPherson's insides dropped into his shoes when he heard Bishop Able say...

"Mary, where's Sarah?"

Mr. McPherson just shook his head as he ambled back to the bar with Ms. Loy right behind him. This was just too much for him. First was Victoria's death, and now Rachel's social suicide.

He should have known they were in trouble when he fired Olivia for her blatant disrespect earlier this evening. She could be one vengeful witch when she wanted to be. But that was nothing. After all, actresses come, and they go. They could always find another actress.

But now that the Conservative Baptists had learned of Rachel's friends' dubious faults and backgrounds, they were leaving, and they were taking their money with them. No money meant there would be no play. And worst of all, his relationship with Bishop Able was now strained. He knew in his bones that Mackenzie had met up with and made off with the Bishop's daughter.

What had happened? This night began with so much promise. Only hours ago, everyone was happy. Mr. McPherson looked at the clock as he poured himself and Ms. Loy another drink. It was 12:03 am. The New Year had come and gone; no one had even noticed. Where was the countdown? Where were the yells and kisses? The cheers and toasts? The only thing that had happened was the slow exodus of the guests towards the door.

CHAPTER 11

While Paul was wreaking havoc on Rachel's future, James and Alex bickered, and Rachel was enjoying her apparent triumph, Mackenzie and Sarah were still sitting on the piano bench. They were in a perfect little bubble of sound and sex appeal. They talked about everything in hushed little private whispers. The music was soft and felt like a caress. Sarah talked about her father, her work, and the arts. Mackenzie spoke about the music, his dreams, and his secret desire to be a conductor. It was perfect, they were so alike and so different. Mackenzie was a perverted but lovable master of debauchery. Sarah was a debutante. But they worked. Their love of music joined them, the one element that broke all barriers of race, class, and education. It seemed...that they could learn to love each other.

This girl is different... I think I could actually fall in love with this one. She has everything you could want: class, beauty, and brains... Then Mac shook himself out of it. Oh, come on, you fall in love? Don't be an idiot!

But the thought was planted, and just when Mackenzie talked himself out of pursuing Sarah—she was a minister's daughter for the love of God—he suddenly blurted out the last thing he wanted to.

"Look, Sarah, it is getting kind of noisy in here. Could I have the pleasure of buying you a coffee or something? I know this great little cafe around the corner. It stays open all night for the insomniacs and truckers."

Sarah smiled slightly. *How random. Who said things like that?* Most people would find that strange and juvenile, but it made Sarah laugh. She giggled as she looked up at Mackenzie. "Well, I came here with my folks, I really shouldn't leave."

Mackenzie melted at those eyes, and then he glanced around and noticed Frank McPherson talking to a distinguished older gentleman. "Is that gentleman talking to Mr. McPherson, your father?"

Sarah glanced in the direction Mackenzie was looking and nodded her head yes.

"Well, we'll have a quick cup of coffee and race back here before your family misses you," Mackenzie suggested. "When I said around the corner, I really do mean around the corner, we could walk."

Sarah thought it over. Mackenzie grinned. He could see the thoughts turning in her head. She was amazing—the ancient Greek muse of song and poetry in human form. She was beautiful, and when she was with him, he knew he would never have a problem composing. She made him want to write ballads with fluffy, sugary sonnet lyrics. Mackenzie shook his head.

Pull it together, Mac. She is way too good for you. No, she's too good for anybody; she's perfect. That thought actually hurt far more than it should have.

"Well, I guess that's okay. I don't see the harm in that." Sarah agreed with a gentle smile.

"Great, let's get going." Mackenzie was happy, ecstatic, and blissful.

Sarah and Mackenzie walked arm in arm to the table where the party's guests laid their coats and hats. Mackenzie asked Sarah which coat was hers, and she pointed to a red single-breasted full-length topcoat. Mackenzie picked the coat up and held it by the shoulders.

"Sarah, may I have the honor?"

Sarah smiled and turned her back to Mackenzie so he could help her put on her coat. When she had it on, she turned around to face him.

"Sarah, you are a beautiful woman." The compliment was so genuine and heartfelt that it even shocked Mackenzie. Mackenzie coughed, feeling slightly embarrassed that he may have overstepped himself. He put on his silk top hat and fastened his cloak over his shoulders.

Sarah smiled at Mackenzie and held out her arm to him. "Shall we?"

"I am at your service, Ma'am." Mackenzie took her arm in his.

It felt right and natural, and their strides were just even enough to be comfortable—the way it should be. Then they walked out of the Condo, took the elevator to the ground floor, and strolled to the cafe at the corner of the street.

The café was a quaint little shop. It had corded off space for outdoor tables and chairs, but, being winter, they had all been brought in for the season. Inside, the café was brightly decorated for the season in silver, gold, and blue, but at this late hour, its lights were lowered for a more romantic mood. A somewhat fairly large group of yuppies had already gathered to celebrate the New Year; they spoke merrily of love, stocks, and hopes for the New Year. Cheerful Christmas music still played over the loudspeaker, creating an air of peace and love.

Mackenzie and Sarah found an empty booth in the back when they entered the cafe. Sarah unbuttoned her topcoat and turned her back to Mac. He assisted her out of the coat and hung it on the small coat hook that protruded from the frame of their booth. Mackenzie began to unfasten his cloak clasp.

Sarah smiled and laid her hands on his. "Mac, you are really something special."

Mackenzie blushed again, wishing he could call on his normal suave and savvy. He smiled at her and thought, *Man, you're wonderful; I don't want this evening to end*. But Mackenzie just put on a comical, lopsided grin and said, "I think you need to get your eyes checked."

Sarah's smile faded. "I don't think so. I have excellent eyesight. I can see right through your act, Mr. Mackenzie, and I like it."

Mackenzie gestured for Sarah to sit down. As she did, he removed his cloak and hat and laid them where he had placed Sarah's coat. He then sat down next to her and motioned for a waitress to serve them.

When the waitress arrived, Mackenzie looked at Sarah. "Sarah, this is my treat, so the sky's the limit."

Sarah beamed at Mackenzie, looked at the waitress, and ordered a double espresso. Mackenzie ordered the same. Then the waitress left. Sarah looked into Mackenzie's eyes and curiously found herself within them.

"I can't understand this. I have only just met you and know next to nothing about you, but I feel like I have known you forever." She confessed, at a loss for this feeling growing within her.

Mackenzie returned her stare and shared the same intensity. "Thank goodness, I wasn't the only one thinking that this evening. I've been calling you my muse all night." He could feel her retaking his arm and holding it tight against her.

"Your muse? That's a high compliment from a musician. So, tell me about yourself, Mr. Mackenzie." She requested.

"Please call me Mac. All my friends do. Besides, there isn't too much to tell Sarah. I am the only son of an only son of a Jewish mother," Mac joked. "I'm not much more than that. You already know I'm a musician, but enough about me, what about you?"

Sarah laughed and replied in like manner. "I am the only daughter of a Baptist father. He's a

Bishop. I have a passion for History and European Art History. It was my father who got me interested in that. I received my doctorate in European Art History at age twenty-five. I've learned to speak German, French, Spanish, Latin, and Greek. I like most types of music, but I love early R&B and Gospel music. I enjoy reading Goethe, Voltaire, Maya Angelou, and Greek Mythology."

The waitress returned and placed coffees on the table in front of Sarah and Mackenzie, but they hardly noticed.

"Wow! That's some resume." Mackenzie chuckled. He was very impressed with her achievements. "So why are you hanging out with a guy like me again?"

"Now it's your turn, Graf Mackenzie Jefferson von Hallbach-Eunbank." Sarah's giggle seemed to make the place sparkle.

Mackenzie knew he was going soft and probably insane. This was the stuff of sappy romance novels. He had always liked erotica, but this couldn't be right, could it?

"My name is my resume. There's really nothing more to tell." Mackenzie sighed, slightly abashed. "I'm a simple guy with expensive tastes."

But Sarah would not be so easily put off and insisted on knowing everything about Mackenzie. So, for the first time in his life, he told her the unvarnished truth about himself. He told her about his mother, who was from an old aristocratic family from Konigshauffen. She converted to Judaism before marrying Mac's father, a civil servant from a southern horse ranching family.

He told her about the car crash that killed his parents when he was five, and how he had to live with his father's parents on their horse ranch until he was thirteen. After his father's parents died, Mackenzie was sent to live with his mother's father, who lived in Konigshauffen. Mackenzie explained how his grandfather had doted on him because he was the only grandchild he had. Mackenzie told her about how he started in music and his passions for jazz and history.

But Mackenzie began to feel that he had monopolized the conversation, and he started to change the subject when Sarah looked at Mackenzie, and she asked...

"Mac, what time is it?"

Mackenzie pulled out his pocket watch. "It's 11:57."

Sarah looked worried. "We had better get back to the party."

Mackenzie sighed and nodded in agreement. As they stood up, someone at the bar yelled..."10 seconds to midnight!"

Sarah grinned and cocked her head to the side. "11:57 huh?"

Mackenzie looked slightly embarrassed as he looked down at his watch. "I knew I should've had this watch serviced."

Mackenzie and Sarah looked into each other's eyes as the patrons in the cafe counted down the remaining seconds of the old year. Then everyone in the cafe yelled, "MIDNIGHT! HAPPY NEW YEAR!"

At that moment, as if of the same mind, Mackenzie and Sarah embraced and kissed each other with a passion neither of them had ever felt before. It was like their first kiss erased all thoughts of the party and even time itself. Then, as if by mutual consent, they grabbed their coats and left the cafe arm in arm.

Mackenzie hailed a cab, and before either of them realized it, they were in the Foyer of Mac's Penthouse. Mackenzie embraced Sarah, not wanting to lose this magnificent woman whom he had found.

"Sarah, I want you to know that you are the most beautiful woman in the world, and that I have never wanted a woman as badly as I want you. But this is up to you. I never thought I'd say this but... It's your decision if you want..."

Mackenzie was silenced by Sarah's fiery kiss. She unfastened the clasp to Mac's Cloak and let it fall to the floor. Mackenzie needed no more encouragement; barely a second later, he had unbuttoned Sarah's topcoat. She growled playfully at him as he picked her up and bridal carried her towards his bedroom in between kisses hotter than the surface of the sun.

Once in his room, Mackenzie lowered Sarah back on her own two feet. Sarah yanked

Mackenzie's tie, pulling him in for another flaming kiss. He smelled like expensive cigars and tasted like even more expensive alcohol. Sarah grinned as she untied Mackenzie's tie, tugged it off, and tossed it to the floor. The blue cross around his neck soon joined it. She trailed her lips across Mackenzie's neck as he slowly pulled Sarah's hair out of its curly bun. Her hair fell, cascading around her shoulders, and she giggled into his neck.

Sarah looked up at Mackenzie, her eyes darkened by lust, and she pulled his sash over his head. Sarah shivered when Mackenzie reached around her and unzipped her dress. His hands were so warm against her. They were rough, though, calloused from years of playing music.

Mackenzie stood in awe as the dress slithered off Sarah's body and to the floor. He wanted to tell her she was beautiful...perfect...a goddess, but all he did was blink. Finally, he uttered the stupidest thing he could think of.

"Hallelujah!"

Sarah burst into a fit of giggles so bubbly that she thought she would cry. She wiped her eyes and pressed her lips onto Mackenzie's with renewed fire. He was so funny...so talented... so wonderful.

Mackenzie was grateful for it. He had no idea how he was going to live that down. Mackenzie ran his hands down Sarah's back, raising goosebumps along her spine. Mackenzie grinned, with a deft flick of his wrist, and with two fingers, he unfastened the clip of Sarah's bra.

Sarah grumbled as she fumbled with the irritatingly small buttons of Mackenzie's vest and his platinum shirt studs. She wanted the damned shirt gone.

Mackenzie slid her bra off in one smooth motion down her arms and then to the floor. Her breasts were perfect. Sure, they weren't huge, but that wasn't the issue. It was their shape and feel. They were like velvet, and they fit in his hands like they were made for them.

Sarah unfastened his trousers and slid his suspenders off his shoulders. She purposefully unzipped his pants and let them fall to the floor.

While she did, Mac took in her perfectly sculptured body. He grinned with all the excitement of a boy on Christmas morning. He lifted Sarah's near-naked body onto the bed and gently placed her down. His wanting eyes scoured every inch of her perfect being.

"Sarah, you are an angel." He gushed happily.

"Well then, come here," She smiled at him and wiggled her forefinger in a come here manner. "and tarnish my Halo."

CHAPTER 12

Morning came slowly for Mackenzie and Sarah. Mackenzie woke, rubbing the crust out of his eyes, to find Sarah lying on her side next to him. Her smile was wistful and content. It wasn't embarrassed, ashamed, disappointed, or regretful; it was…wonderful.

Mackenzie ran his hand along Sarah's cheek. "Is everything okay?

Sarah nodded, gracing Mackenzie with a gentle peck on the lips. "Just fine."

"I had a good time last night," Mackenzie told her honestly.

Good was putting it milder than hot sauce with no jalapeño. It had been amazing, but he didn't know how Sarah would react.

"So did I," Sarah sighed dreamily. She looked at Mackenzie, and she felt shame. "I have never done this before."

"Done what?" He asked, wondering what she was thinking. *Is she regretting last night?*

"Met a guy and followed him to bed on the same night," Sarah told him, and she sighed again with happiness and contentment. Last night was marvelous, and too hard to put into words.

"I hope you don't regret this little slip of propriety. Because I most certainly don't. I'd slip all the time if you were involved."

"You're right. The crazy thing is I don't." Sarah's gratified smile slowly faded.

That's weird. My world brightens when she smiles and darkens when she frowns. How sad is that? I'm an idiot. "Neither do I, Sarah."

"I thought that was pretty obvious." A ghost of a smile returned, and Sarah shook her head, leaning on Mackenzie's shoulder. It was comfortable there.

Mackenzie blushed. Was it that obvious that he was a lech? "No, I wasn't referring to that..."

"I was." Sarah's grin was bright, and it hid lust and longing. Mackenzie was hit with a wave of desire so strong he thought he would choke. *How did she do that?*

"No, what I meant was...what we...what...what happened last night was something really special." Mackenzie tried to say, as he tripped miserably across his words. He hated himself for the confused floundering he was doing. *Come on, man, pull it together. Where are your witty one-liners? Where is my charm and my perfectly placed innuendos? Shoved out the window with my dignity, most likely.*

"There's an original line." Sarah interrupted her new lover with a wry grin. "How unlike you to use a cliché."

Mackenzie chuckled. "I won't argue the originality, but the meaning is genuine." His smile faded as he added. "Sarah, I know you won't believe this, but I have never felt this way about a woman before."

Sarah hugged Mackenzie. It was sweet and romantic, but she knew it was also true, which scared her a bit. *This isn't supposed to happen this fast, is it? Does love at first sight even happen in real life?* "Mac, you are full of originality this morning."

"I know I must sound as corny as Kansas, but it's the truth." Mackenzie said, with a slight edge to his voice. "I can't really explain it, but you get the general idea."

"You're cute when you're flustered?" Sarah said, smiling. She did get the picture, but she wanted him to say it. She wanted to hear him say the words she never knew could be said in only a day.

"Well, I guess what I'm trying to say is that I don't want this to end. I am in love with you."

"How can you know you love me in one night, Mac?" She had wanted him to say it, but actually hearing it was a shock. It sounded so heavy, so powerful, so strange.

"Do you really want to know?" Mackenzie asked, sitting up indignantly.

"Yeah, I would Graf von Vachamacallit." Sarah's playfulness made Mackenzie a little less petrified about what he was about to say, but not much less.

Mackenzie frowned and he was beginning to grow exasperated "Look Sarah, I know I am no great prize; but let me tell you a few things about me, I am as honest as the day is long, I am doggedly loyal to the people I care about, and I always keep my promises."

"Mac, I know you're a good man." Sarah now sat beside Mackenzie. "I could tell that last night…"

"How?" Mackenzie interrupted her with a sigh.

"I have my ways;" she smiled at him slyly. "but how do you know that you love me, especially since we have known each other for less than twenty-four hours?"

"Sarah, frankly, I don't know…" Sarah started to speak, but Mackenzie cut her off. "Sarah, please let me finish. I know that I am in love with you. I can't explain how I know; I just know that I am. As we talked at the party and the pub last night, I kept thinking that this lady is different; she has everything a guy could want or imagine. I told you that I'd been calling you my muse, and I wasn't lying. When I look at you, I hear music. I see notes flying past me at a million miles a minute. Symphonies and orchestras, you define that for me. I meant it when I told you that it felt like I had known you forever. I have never felt that kind of connection with anyone before. I know it's hard to believe, but I'm being honest here. I meant it when I told you last night that you are an angel. It was not said in a fit of passion or lust. I never play around with words like love. You've become my muse."

Sarah stared into Mackenzie's eyes, and somehow, she knew he meant every word he said. It was puzzling, baffling, and frightening how honest his eyes were. How much she felt his passion behind those words. She could only imagine the passion in his music.

"Mac, you're wonderful too, but I..." She began.

Mackenzie interrupted her again. "Kiddo, I love you. Good heavens, I know this is really sudden, I know that what I am saying defies all common sense, but does love ever really make any sense?"

Sarah kept staring into Mackenzie's eyes, unable to speak. This love affair defied all common sense. There was no reason to love this scruff yet sophisticated piano man, but she did. And no matter how she looked into his eyes, she always found herself there. This feeling of being whole and complete was something she had never felt in her life. Not even when she was granted the esteemed position of history professor at the university. Never in her life had she ever felt this overwhelming joy. This indescribable feeling was a little unfathomable. And although her head said take it slow, her heart was more than ready to make the leap.

"I love you too, Mac," Sarah replied, in the same bewildered, breathless tone. "I love you, because until last night, the only things I've ever lived for were my books and my faith. But now, now I know why a man leaves his mother and father and cleaves unto his wife. For the first time in my life, I honestly feel complete."

"Sarah Rebecca Able, would you be interested in doing me the honor of being Graffin Sarah Rebecca von Hallbach-Eunbank?"

Sarah was astonished, but before she could stop herself, she said. "Yes...but not today."

"Well, I didn't mean right now," Mackenzie replied with a small chuckle. "I'd like you to know what kind of mess you're getting yourself into."

Mackenzie embraced and kissed Sarah again, as if to seal the deal. After that kiss, Sarah beamed at Mackenzie and then chose to seal the deal in her own way.

CHAPTER 13

Before Sarah left Mackenzie's place, Mackenzie insisted on making breakfast for her. They ate breakfast and conversed in the eat-in kitchen of Mackenzie's penthouse. When they had finished breakfast, Sarah hugged Mackenzie and pecked him on the lips.

"Mac, I really have to go." She sighed, missing him already.

Mackenzie returned the kiss. "I know," he smiled, etching her glowing face in his memory. I don't like it, but I know."

"Mac, I'll be back, " she promised him. However, I need to see my folks, and they will want to know where I disappeared, too."

Mackenzie looked very serious. "I understand, but do you want me to tag along. I don't want your parents to think I'm..." Sara pressed a single finger to Mackenzie's lips and silenced him.

"Don't worry, Mac, you'll have to meet my folks soon enough, but right now, I had better see them myself." She smiled at Mackenzie to assure him that everything would be okay.

Mackenzie had never seen anyone smile so much, and he swore he would try his hardest not to make her frown. "I'll have the doorman downstairs call a cab for you, " he said, heading to the phone. Mackenzie picked up the telephone on the kitchen wall and dialed.

"Good morning, Meyer. This is Mac Eubank. Yes, that's right in penthouse #4. Please have a cab standing by at the front door. Thank you, Meyer. She'll be down presently."

Mackenzie hung up the phone and gave Sarah a wolfish grin. He pinned Sarah to the wall and kissed her passionately. His hand slipped around her waist as he held her in his arms. Sarah allowed this **extra** attention, but then she pushed Mackenzie away.

"I have to go," She insisted. "Goodbye Mac.... but I'll be back to take you up on that."

Mackenzie released her, opened the door, and escorted her to the elevator. He gave her one last kiss before the doors closed.

"Sarah," He held the doors open a little longer.

"Yes, Mac." She smiled.

"I love you." He confessed.

Her beaming smile turned mischievous. "I know." She gently pushed Mackenzie away so that the doors would close.

Mackenzie watched the elevator doors close on his ladylove. He watched the floor numbers light up as she descended. He sighed heavily as he returned to his penthouse.

"Mackenzie Jefferson Eubank, how could you do this?" He scolded himself. "How could you fall so hopelessly in love?"

Sarah exited the elevator on the ground floor, and a short man in a green doorman's uniform greeted her.

"Mornin', Ma'am. Are you from Mr. Eubank's place?"

Sarah nodded, and the doorman led her to the awaiting cab. She got in the cab and gave the cabbie her address. The cab dropped her in front of her parents' house. She walked up the walk to the front door, unlocked it, and walked into the foyer. She gently closed the door. So as not to make any noise. She started to hang her coat in the coat closet, but she was startled to hear…

"Young lady, where have you been?" Bishop Able's question came off as the start of an interrogation, and Sarah knew it was coming.

"Father, please don't get angry, but I've met someone." Sarah strolled into the den with her head held high. She was a grown woman and didn't need to be afraid of her daddy anymore.

"Have you now? And may I assume that you are just now coming from his place?" Bishop Able took a seat behind his large work desk.

"Yes, father," Sarah answered him truthfully. "You can assume that, but isn't it better if I told you I just came from his place?

"Sarah!" Bishop growled disapprovingly as his eyes zeroed in on her.

"Father, please. I'm not a little girl anymore."

Sarah faced her father on equal terms. She wouldn't be afraid of him right now. She needed to get her point across, and she wasn't about to let him bully her. Sarah tightened her eyebrows into a fierce line as she stared him down.

"Obviously!" Bishop Able scoffed at her and rolled his eyes.

"Father! That was inappropriate. I'm perfectly old enough to make my own choices."

"Don't you father me, you left the party without saying a word. You didn't call to tell us where you were going and stayed out all night! We were worried about you!"

"I'm sorry, Father. I'm sorry I left without a word. I'm sorry I didn't call." Sarah apologized honestly. She was upset with herself for making her parents worry. She loved them. "But I'm not sorry I stayed out all night, that was my choice."

"Then what manner of man has set your heart in fast-forward?" Sarah knew that one. It was her father's *You'd better-answer-me* tone. He had done it since she was a child. He had used it in the pulpit. "What's the name of this knave?"

"Knave? Seriously?" Sarah just shook her head at her father's vocabulary. "He isn't a knave. He's a count."

"A count? Who is this man, and where does he come from?" Bishop asked, leaning forward and propping his elbows up on his desk.

"Graf Mackenzie Jefferson von Hallbach-Eunbank from the Kingdom of Konigshauffen." Sarah said. She was proud of Mac's history…of his class. She was proud of him.

"Gazuntight," Bishop Able scoffed at her with a chuckle. "However, a name is but a name and can change as one wills it. Again, I ask you, what kind of man is he?"

"He's a gentleman. He's a well-traveled man, and he is a musician." Sarah explained calmly and patiently. "He also has quite a sense of humor."

"I would meet this well-traveled gentleman musician." The Bishop said sternly.

"Alright, I'll invite him to dinner." Sarah walked over to his bookcase and ran her fingers over the spines of his books.

"I would have him make an honest woman of you," The Bishop said, as he stood to pack his briefcase for the day. "But not before I've met him."

"Father, I love him with all my heart. But I will not marry him, at least not yet. He and I both have other things to do before we settle down."

Sarah was still young and working on her professorship. She had no time to get married; she had work to do now.

"Then I take it last night was a down payment on your future plans?" The Bishop was still upset, but now he was more irritated than angry. "I still wish you had told us you were leaving."

"Dad?!" Sarah hid her feverish, red face in an open book that she held in front of her. "Don't say things like that!"

"Bring him here to stand before me, to meet me man to man, and I may yet give you my blessing." The Bishop finally smiled. *I can't believe it. My little Sarah is grown, and if she wanted to be serious with a man, she can. But really, sleeping with a man she just met.*

"You won't kill him?" Sarah placed the book back on the shelf before turning to glare, specifically at her intimidating father.

"I won't kill him...physically." Bishop Able gave her daughter a smirking grin.

"Thank you, Daddy." Sarah gushed happily, as she rushed forward to hug her father. "You're gonna love Mac."

"Mac? Wait a minute, not Mackenzie Eubank? That piano playing wolf?!" The Bishop pushed his daughter away to hold her at arm's length.

"That's him." Sarah nodded. "Who did you think I meant?"

"I thought you meant a gentleman. Mac's a lounge lizard...and a drunk.

"He's a musical genius," Sarah retorted, as she leapt to Mackenzie's defense. True she had only just met him, but she wouldn't stand by and let her father insult him. "And he is one of the sweetest men I've met."

"He's a womanizing wolf and an alcoholic. He's lying to you." He shook a disapproving finger in his daughter's face like she was a child. "I'll not have my little lamb devoured by him. You are forbidden to see him again."

"Oh, now that's not fair." Sarah swiped his finger out of her face and slammed her own into his chest. "Now see here, Father, you're being condescending and judgmental! You haven't even met him yet!"

"I saw enough of him last night! He's had dealings with Olivia Reed, and if last night was any example of his past relationships, they don't last long, and they don't end well!" The Bishop ranted, as he had handed down the harsh, critical judgment on a man he had never even spoken to.

"Oh, stop it! Father, I'm an adult! I love him and will still see him if and when I want."

Sarah turned her back on her father just like when she was a teenager. *If he can act childish and petty, then so could I. I'll talk to him when he is ready to be real and mature about this.*

"Not while you live under my roof. I won't allow it, Sarah. He is a horrible match for you. There are better men than him at your University. Why not date one of them?"

"If I can't live under your roof, then I'll live under his." Sarah folded her arms in defiance across her chest and glared at her father. "I'm sure Mac wouldn't mind it."

"I will not have you in a common law union with this man." The Bishop declared, again raining down disapproval with his waggling finger in Sarah's face.

"Then I will make you this deal. If he and I are allowed to date for the next seven years, and at the end of those seven years, he is still in love with me. You will concede that he is a good man and give him pardon for his past misdeeds."

"And if he dares break your heart before the time has ended, then I will break him in two, and you will promise me never to see him again?"

"Deal," Sarah unfolded her arms and stretched out her hand to her father.

"Done then." The Bishop agreed, firmly shaking her hand.

"You'll see, father. He'll vindicate himself." Sarah smiled happily. And he will impress you."

"And you will tell him none of this." The bishop ordered, letting his full pulpit power onto his daughter. "I would see his true colors for myself."

"As you wish. But you know more than anyone that love can change a man. You, yourself, were a bit of a shady character until Mother's love ended your pain. And look at you now, a Doctorate and a Baptist preacher. Who would have bet on you back then?"

Bishop Able allowed himself to reminisce as his daughter's words rang in his ears. "Alright, you win." With a knowing smile, the Bishop relented as he remembered his past deeds. "If he truly makes you happy, bring him round for dinner tomorrow night. And if I like the mettle of this man, then you have my blessing."

"Thank you, Daddy." Sarah gladly hugged her father.

She was so glad that she had won him over. Because if he still disapproved, there was nothing to do but run away with Mackenzie, and she didn't want to hurt her father like that. But she also knew, deep down, that Mackenzie was the one.

"It's so hard for a father to let go of his little girl, and to acknowledge that she's all grown up." Bishop Able ran his fingers through her hair.

"Father, no matter where I go or what I do, I will always be your little girl."

"That's my girl... but it's not true. You're going to be someone's wife one day... and then someone's mother." He sighed, acknowledging the passage of time. "You'll always be my daughter, but you won't be my little girl for much longer."

"At least until the day you die, and then I can do whatever I want, right?" The sly grin was not lost on her father.

It felt good not to be fighting. And it looked like she might be treated like an adult now. The Bishop laughed out loud as he made his way to the front door.

"Sarah, I may be dead and gone, but I will always watch over you," He rubbed the right side of her face and pinched her nose. Was she too old for it? Yes! Did she still love it? Also, yes! "By the way, good luck telling your mother where you've been. I've got work to do at the office. Bye."

Bishop Able quickly kissed his daughter goodbye and closed the front door, just as Mary, Sarah's mother, entered the room.

"Dad!" Sarah yelled.

"There you are, Sarah. Where have you been? I've been worried about you."

Sarah sighed and prepared for the scolding she knew she would receive. Explaining this would be painfully slow, and her mother would not like it. Maybe she should call the paramedics now, because when she told her mother where she had been all night, she was sure her heart would stop.

"Ah, hi mom."

CHAPTER 14

Rachel woke up, blinded by bright sunlight, in James' guest bedroom. No, she woke up naked in James' guest room. Then the sheets rippled around her, and she noticed a naked Ryoji right beside her. Ryoji squirmed, trying his hardest not to wake up yet. Rachel smiled, remembering the magic of last night. She and Ryoji had retired early.

**

Rachel, still giggling and intoxicated, led Ryoji to James' guest bedroom. Ryoji patiently waited as Rachel turned on the stereo and chose music appropriate for the evening. The sweet, mellow sounds of a piano and sax filled the room, setting a heady, intimate mood with the melancholy piano and soulful saxophone.

"The shadows fall and spread their mystic charms, in the hush of night, while you are in my arms. I feel your lips so warm and tender, my one

and only love. You fill my eager heart with such desire, Every kiss you give sets my soul on fire, I give myself in sweet surrender, my one and only love."

The high female voice sang, injecting all her emotions into the lyrics.

Rachel could almost feel the singer crying in joy for her lover. Rachel took Ryoji in her arms, lifting his delicate chin. She looked into his eyes, pools of wild, stormy desire, and kissed him. His lips were sweet like "strawberries and cool whip", was that his lip gloss? Or had he partaken of the dessert tray this evening? The kiss started with soft, gentle prodding. Testing the stormy waters, then as tingling sparks of desire ebbed through them both. Their desire became an intense tsunami of emotions. Ryoji returned Rachel's kiss, making intense, knowing demands of her lips. He pulled at Rachel's tongue as if trying to steal it and her strength from her. This time, Rachel decided oxygen was an unnecessary trifle as Ryoji stole her breath.

Rachel's mind was spinning in a delicious vortex of pleasure. She pulled Ryoji over to her and dropped him into her lap. He straddled her, entangling his perfectly manicured right hand in her jet-black hair. He pulled it lightly, drawing Rachel back to him for another powerful kiss. Rachel's hands wandered, drifting across soft, smooth skin. She'd never noticed how good Ryoji smelled. It was like candy and chocolate, decadence...sweet, delicious, and mostly bad for you. Rachel's questing hands coursed across Ryoji's bare shoulders and down his sleek back till she found the zipper to his dress just under his shoulder blades. She pulled it down, the soft ZZZZing sound making the pretty boy shiver with want. She slipped his dress down over his shoulders.

Ryoji snuggled closer to Rachel leaving deep sucking kisses on her neck. He loved her neck; it was so tasty. Rachel smiled, knowing that she would have hickies marks to explain tomorrow. Ryoji looked up into Rachel's eyes; they were as black as coal, but held an unusual sparkling luster that shone like the stars in heaven.

Rachel planted hot kisses down his neck, to his shoulder's edge, and back again. Ryoji sighed under her touch. She ran her hands over his back and down his spine. Rachel pulled his dress down lower and lower, until he had to rise up on his knees to slide out of it. Rachel smiled bashfully as she looked upon Ryoji's naked form.

"So that's what you've been hiding under your dresses, huh?" Rachel's tease was light and had the edge of a genuine compliment. "Washboard abs and a great yule log."

Rachel stood up, wanting to caress his skin. But Ryoji pushed her back into a sitting position and straddled her lap once again.

"Now it's your turn," Ryoji purred into Rachel's ear. "What are YOU hiding under your ill-fitted suits?"

Ryoji sat there, grinning at Rachel like a cat with canary feathers in its mouth. It was victorious, triumphant, smug, and so sexy. Rachel's deep, glinting eyes and her wicked smile dared him to make a move. She was challenging him to do something...to take control. He teasingly caressed her lips with his, prying open the buttons on her topcoat. Rachel watched with amused anticipation as Ryoji undressed her. His fingers flew over the buttons with deft skill, and his mouth captured her tongue with passion. Next, he removed her tie, snapping it like a miniature whip, before tossing it away absently.

Oh God! He's good. Rachel thought, as Ryoji's hands ran along her blazing body.

Her vest was pulled back and off. Rachel thought it had ended up on the fan, but she didn't care. Rachel lifted his chin and kissed him. Ryoji blushed and fluttered his eyes, undoing one button of her white dress shirt. He continued button after button, letting his tongue run down her skin until her shirt lay on the ground next to her coat. Rachel shuddered and panted as her bra was flung to the floor. Ryoji gently pushed Rachel onto her back and straddled her stomach. Rachel thought he looked powerful and dangerous, and that just made her want him more. She had never seen Ryoji be so dominant. He leaned forward and kissed her breasts, skillfully tweaking her nipples with his tongue.

"Do you want to continue?" The question was a seductive whisper into her skin. His now male voice carried through her body and made her whimper.

"Oh, yes."

"Then, this dance, I will lead." He smiled, and he unzipped her pants.

**

Rachel stretched and rolled her neck. But she just had to smile, too. Everything was just as it should be. She had her actors, her musicians, and a set designer, but more importantly, she had her money. The Conservative Baptists had loved her script and pledged twice what she needed, but even better than all that, she had Ryoji. Rachel looked down at him as he buried his head under a sheet. He was just so damn adorable. She poked him in the head, and he reluctantly sat up. His hair was flying every which way, and he looked like he needed to sleep for another three hours. She had never known Ryoji wasn't a morning person. Even though they had lived together for eleven years, they had always slept in separate rooms.

"Shall I make you breakfast, my lady, Titania?" Rachel smiled and touched her nose with his.

"Have you learned to cook, my lord, Oberon?" He gave her a questioning look.

"Sort of," Rachel chuckled at their silly play. It was so natural just to be together. She wondered why they had waited so long. *Maybe James is right. Perhaps I am a prude*.

"I'll make breakfast, " he declared, getting up. After being in heaven with you all night, I have no desire to visit the hell that is your cooking."

"I've learned to cook...meat." Rachel sank into the bed, feigning deep insult. She even had the audacity to cross her arms and pout. "I can make hamburgers and..."

"Browning hamburger in a pan isn't cooking." Ryoji put on a fluffy pink robe that had been hanging on the back of the door. "It's profaning the sacrifice of a cow. Beef should not be defiled like that."

"Then let me grill you breakfast instead. I may not be able to cook, but I can grill anything." Rachel's boast was loud and haughty, as she channeled Olivia's self-worth, quickly slipping into a shirt and pants. She ignored the bra for now— no need to put it back on before a shower.

Suddenly, they both heard raised voices and then the sound of something shattering against the wall. Rachel and Ryo came running. Out in the living room, Alex and James were having a very heated discussion as Alex pulled on his stylish, warm wool jacket.

"What do you mean I'm out of the gang?!" James' yell was furious, and his face was puffed and red like a beet. "I'm the one setting up the jobs!!"

"Don't you think we should do something?" Ryoji asked as he stood beside Rachel.

"No," Rachel said, watching the drama with folded arms and a heavy heart. "This is James' business, and James will handle it. It's between him and Alex. It has nothing to do with us. Come on, let's give them some privacy."

As if in answer to her prayer to be somewhere else, the doorbell rang. Rachel went and answered it. It was Paul.

"Good morning," Paul said, a false smile plastered on his face.

"How could you betray me like this!?" James' shrill, girlish shout carried all the way to the front door.

"Or maybe not. Trouble in paradise?" Paul quipped.

Paul was ecstatic. James and Alex were still squabbling with each other. They'd still be far too busy fighting with each other to get it together to help Rachel with her work.

"What's up, Paul?" Rachel asked, glancing back towards James and Alex in the living room.

"Thought I'd come by and invite you to breakfast. I didn't get a chance to properly congratulate you last night before you ran off with your boytoy." Paul scoffed with a wicked grin.

"You fucking traitor!" Alex yelled, loud enough to shake the teetering, precarious modern art sculptures. It also made Rachel flinch.

"Me a traitor! That's rich coming from you! I scope out the layouts. I plan the jobs. You pull off the jobs I tell you to!"

"You don't own me!" Alex yelled back.

"No. Nike does." James shot back. "And so does Olivia, apparently."

"So, I took a little bit of her pie for myself. You and your new friends are safe. Nothing I ever did pointed to them!"

"You take too many chances!" James waved his hands about hysterically.

"Oh, and you don't!" Alex yelled back. "Those dumb asses never figured you for the boss man. That every house that you've decorated was knocked over!"

"Not every house. That'd be damn stupid, and just your style." James shot back. "You wouldn't last two days without me!"

"They never even questioned you, because you're so small and helpless. If only they knew you like I do." Alex scoffed. "Maybe I should let them know."

"You wouldn't dare, you ungrateful, backstabbing, son of a hagfish!" James balled his fists and stamped his foot.

"Hagfish?!" Alex was taken aback, but he had no comeback.

So, Alex raised his hand to strike James, but Ryoji caught him by his wrist and twisted his arm. Rachel grinned to herself. His abs weren't just for show. Despite being slim and feminine, Ryoji was a man and strong enough to hold Alex back if need be.

"You don't want to do that. It's a mistake you will regret." Ryoji told him, sounding fierce and dangerous despite his fluffy pink robe. "Just go."

"Fine." Alex jerked his hand away from Ryoji and seemed to make the very air around him quiver with his anger. "I'm done with him anyway. This partnership is done. From now on, I look out for number one. That means I take what I want from whoever I want."

"Fine!" Tears welled up in James' big, soft eyes. "But don't blame me when you end up in jail, you brainless blobfish!"

"Blobfish! Hell with you! I'm out of here!" Alex tossed the comment over his broad shoulders as he stormed off.

Alex forcefully pushed past Rachel and Paul as he stomped out of the front door. James, Ryoji, Rachel, and Paul just looked on and watched him go. But suddenly Alex turned and said...

"And for the record, yes. I buttered Olivia's bread," Alex squeezed his crotch for effect, "and then I took some." He made a snatching gesture. "She's got plenty of loaves after all. Crazy bitch still doesn't realize that some of it is missing."

And with that last jab, Alex left. All heads turned to James. He was livid, raged in anger, and fled to his room. Rachel was the only one who noticed Mr. Tabby rushing off to comfort James. Mr. Tabby sat outside James' door, meowing to be let in. The cat scratched at the door, mewling and purring. Rachel could almost swear she heard it saying, "Let me in, James. Let me help!"

"You should go and talk to him," Ryoji said, moving into the kitchen to prepare breakfast. Omelets okay? I think I saw some eggs in the fridge when we set up last night."

"Fine, but put some coffee on, though, or I'll never be able to get him to open the door," Rachel told Ryoji. Then she turned to Paul. "I can't join you for breakfast today, Paul. I've got a crisis to take care of here."

A smile spread across Paul's face as Rachel headed into the kitchen. *And this is only the beginning. Act two is coming soon. This is only an intermission. You, the heroine, are in for so much more.*

Paul really had no intention of taking Rachel to breakfast. It was just an excuse to come over and watch her face as her world fell apart.

Suddenly, Mackenzie walked through James' open front door, wearing a gray pinstriped double-breasted three-piece suit, white shirt, and a sharp black tie with a diamond stickpin. He walked over to the couch and plopped down, singing to himself.

"Heaven, I'm in Heaven, and my heart beats so that I can hardly speak, when I seem to find the happiness I seek, when we're dancing together, dancing cheek to cheek..."

As he continued singing, he pulled out his gold pocket watch, glanced at the time, untangled the chain, and then put it back into his vest pocket.

Paul grinned. "Something you want to tell us, Mac?"

Mackenzie looked up, slightly startled. When he walked in, he hadn't even noticed the man leaning against the doorframe. "Who are you again?"

Paul coughed to hide his laughter. "Rachel," Paul piped over the empty room. "Mac's here."

Rachel came out of the kitchen, holding a big cup of coffee. "Hey Mac, how's it going?"

Mackenzie sat up and beamed. "Rachel, you'd better brace yourself, I'm in love," He announced happily. "I even got the first stanza written for your play. It's amazing; it's a black love ballad for the wives."

"Who's the poor victim this time?" Rachel laughed and rolled her eyes at him.

"Why," Mackenzie asked, leering at Rachel. "Are you jealous?" His amused grin almost made Rachel drop the oversized cup of coffee.

"Not a bit, I was just wondering if she has had her shots. She'll need them if she's hanging out with you. A flea collar, too."

A cry of anguish ripped through the living room from James' room. It was a deep, melancholy wail that made Mackenzie flinch, dumbfounded by its mournfulness. Rachel, however, just sighed...heavily.

"What's wrong with him?" Mackenzie asked, his cheerful, dopey smile turned into great concern.

"You've gained and he's lost." Rachel shook her head. "They've known each other for a long time. And now, that ship has sailed."

"So, Alex dumped him?" Mackenzie asked as he sat back and rested his arms on the back of the chair.

"Yep. Sit still, and I'll get to you next," Rachel said as she continued to James' door. "I want you to tell me about the score you wrote." Rachel stood in front of James' door and knocked. "James. James, open up. I've brought you coffee." Mr. Tabby meowed. Rachel nodded at the cat. "Thanks, Tabby-tom, you tell him he's being silly too."

James opened the door; he took the coffee, picked up his cat, and closed the door in Rachel's face with his foot.

"You're welcome," Rachel growled. *How did the cat get priority?* She turned to leave, grumbling about James and his cat, when James opened the door.

"I'm sorry, Rachel. I won't be able to design your sets for you. I don't think I could even design a doghouse right now. I need time to think and figure out what to do next."

"How much time?" Rachel's head and ears perked up.

"I don't know," He replied sheepishly. He looked down at the floor, noticing that Rachel's toes weren't pedicured or painted, and cleared his throat. "A year."

"A year?!" Rachel's eyes widened so big they looked like plates, and she stepped back. *Have you lost your mind?* "Oh, come on, James! He's only one guy. You'll find another partner and then…."

"Only one guy!" James repeated, snapping his fingers in Rachel's face. "You should know how important one business partner can be to another! Companies are made or broken and sold based on good partners. Alex and I have been friends for much, much longer than you and Royko. I trusted him…with everything. I just found out that not only did he have an affair with a woman and steal from her, but he lied to me about it, right to my face, for years. So, what else has he been keeping from me? And don't tell me he's only one guy. After all, where would you be without Ryoko?!"

Rachel looked down the hall at Ryoko, sorry Ryoji, who was still cooking breakfast. He bounced and hummed, shimmying his hips sweetly as he stirred the skillet. Rachel smiled wickedly as she thought about him and his culinary talents.

"Probably a lot thinner, but I just love his spaghetti," James growled at Rachel for her insensitivity, and slammed the door in her face. "Oh, come on, James! You know I was just being silly!" Rachel pawed at the door like Mr. Tabby. "James!"

"I'm only one guy!" That yell was full of spite and hurt. James was not going to talk to Rachel anytime soon. "You'll find another, right!?"

"James!" shouted Rachel. This time, she took to pounding on his bedroom door. "James, I'm sorry! Come on! Don't do this to me! James! Damn it! JAMES!!" She kept banging on his bedroom door.

While all this was happening, Olivia walked into James' open front door. She looked around, obviously looking for Rachel. Paul pointed down the hall. Olivia listened to the argument between James and Rachel and then decided to leave her message with Paul. Mackenzie winced with sympathetic pain as Olivia slapped Paul. She told him something that only he could hear, glared at Mackenzie for good measure, and then left in a tempestuous huff.

Tired of arguing with James, Rachel entered the living room mad and at a loss for what to do. That's when Paul slapped her across the face. Honestly, he was happy that Olivia had given him the excuse. He had wanted to slap Rachel ever since she had entered and won that damnable writing contest.

"What the hell was that for?!" Rachel protested as her hand went up to touch her sore face.

"That was from Olivia," Paul said innocently, and he went over to sit opposite Mac.

"Was she here?" Rachel asked Mackenzie as she rubbed her aching cheek.

"Yes, Cruella has come and gone," Mackenzie said, nodding. "She raced out of here on her broomstick, before somebody could drop a house on her."

"And what's her beef?" Rachel questioned, as she snickered at Mackenzie's analogy.

"You know how nobody walks away from a Mr. McPherson production, even if they don't like their role," Paul informed her, as he again made himself comfortable on James' couch.

"Yeah, that'd be theatrical suicide." Rachel surmised, still rubbing her sore and stinging cheek.

"Well, Olivia didn't walk away." Paul chuckled with delight. "She got fired."

"Whatwhohuhhow!?" It was a jumbled, confused rush, as Rachel's brain seemed to need a reboot. "Wait, WHAT?! When the hell did this happen?!"

"Last night, alcohol filled and mad at you, Olivia gave Mr. McPherson a piece of her mind," Paul explained. He was most happy to fill her in.

"Oh, no." Rachel feared, and she facepalmed herself. She didn't' know Olivia that well, just as an old lover of Mackenzie's, and she knew that her mind was only full of self-loving theatrical over pompous crap.

"Apparently, he didn't like the taste. He fired her." Paul shrugged nonchalantly. "And now she's vowed to ruin you."

Paul watched the emotion drain from Rachel's face. *This is going oh so perfectly. I wish I had remembered to bring a camcorder. I could've taped all this, sold it online, and made a fortune. I could've called it "The Last Days of Rachel Washington."* Paul was still thinking dollar signs when Rachel said...

"This can't be happening." In a heap of shocked disbelief, Rachel fell into a seat next to Mackenzie's. She stared at the floor as if looking for answers, but none were down there.

"That's what I keep telling myself. My luck's too good to be true. I have met the most wonderful woman." Mackenzie told her, with exceeding cheerfulness.

"Really?" Rachel lifted her head to look at him. "So, what's this goddess of yours like, Mac?" The news of his new muse was a happier topic. It was what she needed right now. Besides every play ran into hiccups. She was sure that she could fix this later...when everybody had time to cool down. Her Highness wasn't the only high-caliber actress in town.

"Actually," Mackenzie began, his mood irritatingly chipper, delightful, and content. "She's a full professor of European Art history. She loves Voltaire, Maya Angelou, and Greek Mythology."

"Musical tastes?" Rachel was surprised that Mackenzie had fallen for a girl with depth. Usually, his only requirements were a double D cup size and long hair.

"She is eclectic, but she loves early R&B and Gospel. She's sugar and spice and everything nice." Mackenzie gushed happily. "She's cinnamon brown, with a slim and shapely figure; she sets my soul on fire, and I love every moment of it."

Rachel eyed Mackenzie with a smirk. She wouldn't be surprised if Mackenzie started floating from his happy thoughts. He was smiling from ear to ear and seemed to be bouncing to music in his own head. She wondered if she'd have to tether him like a balloon to keep him in the room.

"Rollie, get the hose. Mac's set himself on fire." Rachel squeezed out the comment between bouts of giggles and belly laughs. "So, what's the name of your new muse?"

"Dr. Sarah Rebecca Able."

"Sarah Able?!" Rachel tried to hide her shock and disbelief. That name hit her like a train going in the wrong direction. "Doctor Sarah Able from the party last night?"

"Yep, Sarah Able, Able-bodied Sarah." Mackenzie's wolfish grin was nowhere near as intense as it used to be. It had an edge of softness to it now.

Oh, you're in trouble now. Frank will kill you if the good Bishop doesn't get you first. Paul thought to himself as he tried to remain deadpan.

"Damn it Mac! Of all the women at the party last night, why the daughter of the richest and most conservative backer that Mr. McPherson has? I thought you swore off church girls! If he pulls his money, I'm dead! There is no play without his money! Oh, when you screw up Mac, you go for the gold!"

"Whoa, Rachel, for once, my intentions are reasonably honorable. I'm meeting her parents this evening to..." Mackenzie sat forward and tried to defend himself from Rachel's barbarous slings.

Rachel just shot Mackenzie a look that silenced him.

"Well, if there's no play, then you don't need sets designed," James muttered, matter-of-factly, walking back into the kitchen with his empty coffee cup. Rachel also shot him a harrowing look and growled at him. "Now, if you'll all be so kind as to go home, I'll try and put my worthless life back together."

"We will," Rachel said, pointing to the kitchen. "Right after breakfast. Ryoji's already started cooking."

"Breakfast will be ready in two minutes," Ryoji yelled from the kitchen.

"Are those your eggs Benedict?" James asked as he delighted in their delicious aroma.

"Yes, they are. Do you have the strength to eat with us this morning?" Ryoji patted James in sympathy. It seemed he was the only one who cared about James' feelings this morning.

"I'll get the plates," James said, still playing the victim.

Rachel groaned as she stood up to go to the table. *This is a fine kettle of fish. One man had lost his best friend, and with it, his inspiration. Another man had found love and...*

"Mac, can you still compose my score?" Rachel asked him sharply.

"Of course, I told you I already got the first stanza," Mackenzie assured her. "I'll show you over breakfast. Besides, I gave you my word, didn't I?"

"You did, but..." Rachel looked pensive, and she kept stroking her chin.

"But what, I can compose any part of your play that you can give me from where Elaine falls in love with her mark, to their love affair in Spain, and the happy ending," Mackenzie spoke with a new confidence that Rachel had never seen before. She could see the notes flashing before his eyes, and she nodded.

"What about my dark and somber parts? Or is your muse too happy and fluffy at this time?" Rachel was still steaming with anger, but if Mackenzie came through, then it could start looking up again.

"Let's not talk about your dark and somber parts," Mackenzie chuckled at her. "But if you mean the play, I can write those too, and any other blasted thing you throw at me." Mackenzie pointed a thumb proudly at himself. "I've given you my word and will stand by it."

"Well, that is something, I don't have a play, but I've got the tunes for it," Rachel complained, throwing her left hand up into the air, as if throwing something away. "Maybe we'll do a soundtrack for a play that never was."

"Better than nothing at all; at least I haven't let you down," Mackenzie said matter-of-factly.

"Nah, you didn't let me down," Rachel said, her voice softening. "You did me in!" She snapped as she grew angry again. "You just had to seduce the daughter of one of Frank's most influential and conservative backers! If he pulls his money because you've had an affair with his daughter...Damn it, thanks a lot you bloody over sexed Sot!" Rachel ranted as she dropped into a chair at the table.

Mackenzie's jaw tightened. He got up, stormed over to her, turned her chair around, and made her face him.

"Rachel, I fouled up, and I am sorry it may cause you some difficulty. But for the first time in my miserable life, I have found a woman who loves me for who and what I am. I don't know why she does, but I'm not going to question her about it." He told her as he firmly held onto the arms of the chair.

Rachel was hardly listening to him. She was breaking down. *What happened at that party last night? How did all of this happen, right under my nose? Why are the pieces of my perfect world shattering like broken glass?*

"Rachel, I know that all of this seems to be coming at you from all sides...but rest assured, I will do right by Sarah. And you should already know that I will stand by you, my friend; in good times, through the fires of hell, and all the times in between." He lifted her chin and made her look him in the eyes.

Rachel thought for a moment and then sighed heavily. "You're right, Mac, thanks for that at least."

But then another tidal wave of despair hit Rachel like waves against a battered ship. She turned the chair, pulling it out of Mackenzie's hands, and faced the dining room table. She banged her head against the table. **THUMP, THUMP, THUMP**.

"Damn, damn, damn, it's all falling apart. I just got started, and it's all coming to an end." Rachel agonized in disbelief and helplessness.

Mackenzie looked down at Rachel, who seemed inconsolable. He started to speak but then just laid his hand on Rachel's shoulder. Then he turned around and began to leave the apartment. Ryoji saw what had happened and went over to stop Mackenzie.

"Mac, Rachel's just upset..." Ryoji began.

Mackenzie stopped and looked at Ryoji. When he wasn't in a dress...he was different. The man standing before him was definitely not the woman he had met last night. Mackenzie cut Ryoji short and stepped around him so that he could leave.

"It's okay Ryoko...uh Ryoji...ah yeah. I know she's upset right now. I can't blame her for it. But when she calms down, please do me a small favor?" Mackenzie requested, with a slight grin.

Ryoji looked at Rachel and then at Mackenzie. "Sure"

"Just let her know that whatever else breaks loose, I will be right behind her, all the way." Then Mackenzie held out his hand to Ryoji, and Ryoji shook Mackenzie's hand. Mackenzie chuckled as he felt Ryoji's grip. "Ryoji, if you had shaken my hand like that last night, I'd have had no doubts about you." Then Mackenzie looked down at Rachel and said to Ryo. "Take care of her, for me, will you?"

Paul, still seated and enjoying the show, watched Mackenzie leave. He reveled in Rachel's destruction, but resented Mackenzie still pledging his loyalty to her. *And that cross-dressing freak. They're a perfect trio: the loser, the fairy, and the drunk.* Paul sneered.

Ryoji smiled at Mackenzie's retreating back and then went back to finish cooking breakfast. Rachel, on the other hand, was still in her own world of hurt.

"What else can...? No, no, no, let me not even say that." Just then, her cell phone rang. "Crap, too late!" Rachel glared at the small phone on the table. She knew it was bad news. She knew it would make her cry. She had never dreaded a phone call before, but finally she picked the blasted thing up and answered. "Hello, Good morning, Mr. McPherson."

Paul perked up. *This is it, the last nail in her coffin. This is the curtain call for Act Two. This will be the climax of my perfectly scripted living play, the tragic end that will bring about the heroine's fall.* Paul watched her face most intently. He didn't want to miss a thing.

"Yes, Mr. McPherson. No, Mr. McPherson. You're right, Mr. McPherson. I could blame it on the liquor we drank, but my actions were my own, sir, and there's no one else to blame. No, sir. They are my friends, faults and all."

Now, everyone in the room was listening. Each knew that their actions last night had been poor behavior. James was arguing with Alex over business that shouldn't have been discussed in public unless they wanted jail time. Now that he thought about it, they were both very stupid last night. There were hundreds of witnesses.

"Damn." James bit his thumb.

Ryoji had known better, and he had even warned her. But then again, his own actions were not without fault.

I shouldn't have kissed her then. Ryoji thought to himself. *I should have waited until a more appropriate time.*

"No, sir, last night was all my fault. I take full responsibility." Rachel said, trying desperately to remain strong. "Please give the Bishop and his wife my sincerest apologies."

Paul watched as tears fell and sobs were choked back. Rachel fought to remain professional while she spoke to Mr. McPherson, but Paul knew it would only be a matter of time. He could see her hands shaking as she held the phone tightly.

"Yes, Mr. McPherson. I fully understand. You have no choice. I'm sorry I've disappointed...and embarrassed you, Sir."

Rachel hung up the phone and collapsed to her knees. She began to cry uncontrollably. She just couldn't hold it in anymore. She wanted to disappear and never come back. She wanted to sleep for a month... no, what she really wanted was to wake up. To wake up and discover this was some horrible nightmare. Yeah, that's what she wanted. She rocked on her knees, her head to the ground, and she held her shivering sides. She poured out the pain of her heart. The silence in the room hung heavily like the tolling of a death bell.

Suddenly, Paul cleared his throat as he stood to leave.

"Umm, I a...I guess I'd better go. I'm sorry, Rachel. I know it would have been a great play." He said verbally, but he thought. *I should get a*

Tony award for this. The award for best theatrical production goes to......Paul Cartwright!

Rachel stopped crying, looked up at Paul, and in between her sobs, she said, "You should go and see Frank."

"Did he ask for me?" Paul questioned, his face betraying his surprise.

"No, but...I have a feeling he will. Victoria's dead...and now so am I. You're the only heir to the throne now."

Ryoji looked up from laying out the plates as he heard those words from her. He looked at Rachel and then at Paul. Paul's face was sad and solemn, but his body language betrayed his triumph. Rachel was on her knees, crying in pain, and Paul stood there, lording over her. Suddenly, the lights began to flicker off and on.

CHAPTER 15

Today was a beautiful day. The sun was shining its glorious rays across the sky. The full, fluffy white clouds lazily drifted across the blue and endless sky. It was even pleasantly warm for a January morning. It was the kind of day that made people question if it was really winter.

Ryoji put on his best outfit and found Rachel on the balcony of their luxury condo, lying on their only sad and lonely lounge chair. She was staring up at the clouds but wasn't seeing them—she wasn't seeing anything. Her face was void and expressionless. She had lost her smile and her shine. She used to be so quirky and full of life. She used to sit on tables and countertops just to annoy him. She used to hug him and always had a snappy one-liner.

Now she was hollow and cold. The world around her was new, bright, and promised spring, but she was dead and dying in darkness and despair. A despair so dark and deep that she never noticed a worry-filled Ryoji looking down at her.

She looks so helpless, so utterly defeated. She was my knight in shining armor. She treats me like a noble lady of royal blood. She's the only person who makes me feel special and not like some sick freak. With her strength, I was finally able to realize my dream and open my first shop. And with her behind me, I feel like I can do anything, even the impossible. I have to help her. But how does the princess save a knight? I've worked hard to build my clothing empire, and with Rachel's plays to showcase my work, the orders never stopped pouring in. She gives me the strength of a thousand men, and yet I'm her kryptonite. It pains me to see her this way.

"Are you going to be alright?" Ryoji asked her as he gently sat down beside her.

He wrapped his arms around her on the narrow chair. It was supposed to be close and intimate and warm, but it wasn't. She wasn't his Rachel anymore. She was a cold, empty shell of his Rachel. She hadn't even noticed he was wearing her favorite outfit, an A-line pink skirt with the pretty V-neck cardigan and white sweater she had gotten him. Rachel sighed and nodded. Ryoji took her hand in his, gently kissing her fingers.

"Don't worry, Ryoko. I won't go jumping off any bridges."

"Promise?" He gave her hand a worried squeeze. He didn't want to let go of Rachel. She was so very special to him. "Because if you do, I swear I am burying you in the frilliest, pinkest, laciest dress that I have, and you are going to be wearing heels in your coffin."

That had gotten a weak smile out of Rachel. It was short and strained, but it was a smile. She sat up and pulled Ryoko into her lap.

"I give you my word, my lady." She gave Ryoko's ear a gentle nip as she tightened her grip on him. "If I were to die, who would look after you?"

"You're only one guy. I'll find another," Ryoko teased with a smile. "A girl like me only has to bat an eyelash, you know?"

Rachel burst out laughing. It felt good, lifted some of the heavy gloom off her, and allowed her to finally breathe again.

"Alright, I'll go and apologize this afternoon. I was only thinking of myself. I didn't mean for it to sound like that." Rachel smiled at Ryoji. "I'm just no good when it comes to comforting people."

"I beg to differ," Ryoko said, resting her head upon Rachel's chest.

It should have been awkward with him being taller. It should have felt strange curling up in Rachel's lap, but it didn't. He didn't even care that the people walking under the balcony could probably see up his skirt. They sat there for minutes, just watching planes fly by.

"Why don't we go to Australia?" Rachel announced suddenly and out of the blue. "I need a holiday. This is a new year; maybe I should try a new profession. What do you say to raising sea turtles?"

Ryoko shook her head and turned serious eyes on Rachel while she was normal. "How well do you know Paul?" It wasn't a sweet, innocent girlish question. It was an order that Ryoji pulled from his powerful inner self. "Answer me, Rachel."

"OK, you need to pick a voice." Rachel chuckled. "Ryoko or Ryoji?"

"Don't dodge me," commanded Ryoji, as he gave her a flick against her forehead.

"We've been friends since fifth grade," Rachel said, slightly surprised by his seriousness. "True, we may not be as close as we once were, but we're busy people now."

"What would you say…if I told you…I think he orchestrated your fall from grace?"

At first, Rachel didn't answer. She just sat there thinking about it. Then she said, "He who would be king, huh? But, even if he did, my actions were my own. You tried to warn me, but I did it anyway. Rollie, I will not go through life blaming other people for my problems. You told me how it would look, and I did it anyway. I knew Mac would probably get in trouble, and James and Alex are painfully obvious when they're together. I should have thought harder...looked at it from a more business perspective and not just as a party for friends."

"You know, Rachel, for someone so wise in the world of make believe, she who can see plot twists and surprise endings a mile off, you're a 'babe in the woods' in the real world. And you'd be eaten by wolves, if it weren't for me." Ryoji said as he turned around in her arms and kissed her lips. "Don't worry, Robin. I, Maid Marion, will speak to the Sheriff of Nottingham for you."

Ryoji bounced out of Rachel's lap, far more gracefully than any man should be able to, while wearing heels.

"Just don't go promising to marry him to stay my execution." Rachel chuckled as she finally sat up.

"Nah, I don't think he'll have me." Ryoji gave her a smile and a wink. "I'm not the good Bishop's type."

"The Bishop!" Rachel jumped up out of the seat like it had bitten her. "I thought you meant Frank."

"Of course you did, my little babe," Ryoji smirked, and he gently tapped her nose. Then he sauntered away. "Like I said, you're clueless in the real world. Frank has no problem with you...but the Bishop does."

"Rollie." Rachel cried out, and she ran to grab his arm.

Ryoji turned to face Rachel and lovingly caressed the side of her face. "Rachel, you've always been my handsome prince. You've always stood behind me in every move, giving me the strength to move forward and never letting me run away from a fight. Since the day we met, you've saved me time again. This time, let me save you. Let me try on your armor, in a lady's size six."

Ryoji caught Rachel in a kiss and then went inside. Rachel stood in a stunned silence and watched him go, and for the first time in his life, since the day they met, Ryoji didn't look like a damsel in distress, but a determined man of purpose...even if he was wearing a pink skirt with high heels.

CHAPTER 16

Ryoji sat in Bishop Able's office, wearing a stylish black three-piece suit. Wearing a man's suit after years of dresses and heels felt strange. He felt short in his polished black loafers, but they did match his belt perfectly. He wanted to twirl his hair, but it was short and spiky now. He tried to cross his legs and pout, but this wasn't the time.

As he waited patiently for the Bishop to finish his phone call, he looked around the room. Images of the Christian faith: crosses, chapels, and even a lovely portrait of Jesus as a Middle Eastern man, were on the wall behind him. The walls were a lovely warm burgundy, but the office was small and oppressive. His doctoral degrees were hung in a perfectly straight, neat line behind his head. Ryoji read each one. This Bishop was a well-learned man of God. He had a Doctor of Theology and a master's degree in business. He reminded Ryoji of the apostle Paul. He, too, was a learned man of God who had been so devout as to be called a zealot. Hopefully, the Bishop would be easier to talk to.

"I'm sorry, Mr. Sato, church business." Bishop Able apologized as he hung up the phone.

"Quite all right, Bishop Able. I'll not waste your time. I will be quite frank and honest with you." Ryoji tried his hardest not to let his girlish lilt into his soft accented voice. He kept himself rigid and still. "I'm here on theater business."

"I'm sorry, Mr. Sato, but we will not support the arts...this year." Bishop Able stated. He tried to continue, but Ryoji raised his hand and silenced him. That was a feat. Almost no one could silence Bishop Able.

"Bishop Able, there has been a great misunderstanding. Rachel Washington does not deserve your scorn."

"Miss Washington has shown me her colors, of which I do not approve." There was just a hint of condescension, just a thin edge of indignation and righteousness.

"You are mistaken, Sir. Rachel is not a lesbian." Ryoji noticed that the Bishop flinched.

Bishop Able didn't even like hearing the word. Ryoji let the Bishop have a moment before he continued, "The girl that Rachel was kissing was...was me."

"Mr. Sato, I know the difference between a man and a woman."

"Once again, Bishop Able, I must say you are mistaken. I am a fashion designer. I wore the dress to show it off. I wanted her to see my designs for her play."

Half-truths weren't exactly lies, but the Bishop was no fool. Ryoji knew there was no getting out of this without the whole truth being known. Only if he told the truth, he would never wear a dress again.

"The girl in the dress, was you?" The Bishop's unbelief was like a neon sign; it was just that blatant.

"Yes," Ryoji confessed softly.

"So, then she was really kissing a boy." The Bishop said it like a brilliant deduction, almost like he was discovering some great secret.

"Yes." Ryoji nodded.

"No, the illusion was too real. You're a cross-dresser then, aren't you?"

"Yes, but there is a good reason," Ryoji said. He took a deep breath and wished he felt as bold and strong as he did in his dresses. But he didn't. He was nervous and frightened, for himself and for Rachel. But now was not the time for weakness either. After all, Rachel had given him his start; now it was up to him to provide Rachel with hers.

"There can be no reason good enough to profane God's word. I've heard enough." Bishop Able declared as he rose to file the finished paperwork before him.

"Bishop, please! Let me confess my sins to you." Ryoji exclaimed with sincerity.

The Bishop stopped, looked at Ryoji's earnestness, and sat back down. He then looked at Ryoji and saw a frightened young man begging for help. His demeanor softened, and he nodded to Ryoji, promising to listen.

"When I was ten years old, my twin sister and I were in a car accident. A speeding car struck our school bus, and it pushed us off the road. The bus flipped over and rolled over five times before it stopped. A few of the children were lucky and were thrown from the bus. But a lot of them weren't and were trapped inside. The bus caught fire and exploded as the fuel tank burst. More than half the children died that day. My sister was one of them."

At first, Bishop Able was only half listening to him, but now he was all ears, and his heart went out to those poor children who had died.

"Since my sister and I were twins, and her body was so badly burned that they couldn't tell us apart. They put the wrong name on the wrong gurney, and the Doctors told my parents that their son was dead. It was three weeks later before I could leave the hospital. And when I got home, they had already buried me. All my things were stored in the attic, and everything that reminded them of me was gone."

"You never told them?" Bishop Able asked, his harsh, decisive voice now carrying softer tones of remorse.

"I didn't want to hurt them. They seemed so happy that my sister survived. And they didn't seem to worry or care so much that I was gone. "Everything blue was gone, and only the pink remained, and my parents seemed okay with that."

"Mr. Sato, trust me. Parents are never happy to lose a son…or any child. Maybe they didn't want your sister to be unhappy either." Bishop Able comforted him. "Maybe they pretended to be happy for her sake."

"Maybe, but it sure didn't feel that way to me." Ryoji sighed as he let his head rest in his hands and bared his soul. "They were very rigid people, my parents, and they made it hard for me to tell them that they were wrong, that I wasn't my little sister."

"Are your parents still alive?" The Bishop asked, with soft concern.

"No," Ryoji replied calmly. "I lost them twenty years ago."

"And you never thought about changing back? You never thought about becoming a man again?" Bishop Able sat back and folded his hands in his lap.

"I couldn't. I was famous by then. Sato Ryoko was the 'Woman-of-the-hour' in fashion. I wanted to be recognized for my talent and honor my sister. I didn't want to be just another man who designed women's clothes. I couldn't just suddenly be a man in a dress."

"Lots of men design women's clothes." Bishop Able reminded him with a chuckle.

"Name one that isn't gay," Ryoji hackles raised in irritation. The Bishop wasn't getting it.

"And you don't want people thinking you're a catamite?"

"I'm not a boy toy." Ryoji practically snapped at him.

"Oh yes, I can see that being a cross-dresser is better than being called queer." The Bishop smirked, and a small smile crept onto his face.

Ryoji smiled. Bishop Able was a man of staunch religious beliefs, but he also had a sense of humor. That was a good sign.

"Bishop, please, Rachel needs your money. She needs this chance. She gave me my start. Please don't take hers away because of me."

"I have your story, and I guess I can understand it. Can't say I would have done the same if I were in your place, but I know why you did it. But there is no misunderstanding Mac's indiscretion with my daughter or James' obvious sexual preferences." The Bishop reminded Ryoji sternly.

"Mac is a wolf. I can't argue that point. But he is also a good-hearted man. He'd never hurt your daughter. And I know his loyalties, once given, remain true forever. He's no fair-weather friend. I've watched him over the years stand by Rachel through thick and thin. I've talked to him. He is madly in love with your daughter, sir. She may have actually changed him. I've never seen Mac so...content."

"I've already spoken to Mac and Sarah. He knows what I expect of him. I can't understand how or even why Sarah loves him. He is not the man that I would have picked for my little girl. But, I have never seen her as happy as she is with Mac. So, long as that man stays good to Sarah, keeps making her happy, and stays sober around me, then I'll learn to deal with him," The bishop said, his tone becoming more understanding; but then it took on a tone of crossness. "But as for James…,"

"James isn't a homosexual either." Ryoji shook his head no. "He's just a mama's boy."

"He and Alex…their argument…" Bishop Able tried to remind him.

"Was about…artistic differences," Ryoji spoke diplomatically. "Rachel has never really told me about those two. She just said that they've been best friends since they were young. Just like her and Paul."

"Paul was the one who told me that she and her gang of friends were not on the up and up, and it appeared that he was right." Bishop Able sat forward now and talked with Ryoji, man to man.

So, Paul really is our traitor. "But Bishop, were not some of Jesus' most devoted followers reprobates, dregs, and prostitutes?" Ryoji asked sincerely. The Bishop sighed as he thought this over. "If you're going to be a fisher of men, you can't just throw them back because you don't like them. Besides, a good fisherman must know when to reel them in and when to let them run."

"How come you are so knowledgeable about the church?" Bishop Able questioned.

"I once had the pleasure of designing new habits for a convent in Italy. They were sweet and gentle women who opened their arms to everyone, regardless of their station in life or profession. I will always remember Sister Bianca saying that 'Physicians heal only the sick.' And if you think about it, whether people know it or not, the whole world is hurting." Ryoji presented his case most eloquently.

The Bishop sat silently and stroked his tie as he thought things over. Then he gave his verdict. "From now on, you will wear men's clothes. I will allow Mac to date my daughter...for now. And James...once a month, he must attend church. If he comes more, he is welcome; but I will see him once a month." The Bishop proposed.

"Done." Ryoji smiled. He was relieved that he had succeeded.

The Bishop picked up the phone. "Margaret, please get me Frank's office."

"Thank you, Bishop Able." Ryoji stood up to leave and exited the bishop's office.

Ryoji smiled brightly as he walked down the hall and out of the front door. It was a harsh ultimatum, but he could do it. He would do it for Rachel, and hopefully she would make it big.

CHAPTER 17

Ryoji hung his coat on the rack by the door, closing it with the back of his foot. He was weary, tired, and wanted a hug. After dealing with the good Bishop all afternoon, he was drained and felt vulnerable.

"Rachel?!" Ryoji called out.

"Balcony," Rachel answered him, as she flipped the steaks that she was cooking.

The delicious smell of smoked paprika grilling meat wafted from the open balcony door. It didn't smell too burned yet. He shook his head and allowed himself to laugh. Rachel couldn't cook to save her life, but she was a master at the art of grilling. Her steaks were always tender and juicy. Ryoji's mouth began to water just thinking about them.

Ryoji removed his top jacket and vest and undid his tie. The jacket and vest were tossed roughly onto the back of the sofa. He pulled at the buttons on his shirt, unbuttoning them one by one until he could breathe again. Ryoji had never realized how stuffy a suit was. He stepped into the kitchen, intending to head for the balcony door, but his jaw dropped to the floor when he saw what he saw.

"Chikushou! What happened to the kitchen?!"

The kitchen was a disaster. There were scorch marks on the ceiling; it was like a small explosion had happened on the stove. Was the countertop melted? Pots and pans littered the formerly spotless tile floor in various states of destruction. Most of them looked salvageable. Only one word came into his mind ... Rachel.

He composed himself, pulling his hand from in front of his wide-open mouth and taking a deep breath. Then, he joined Rachel on the balcony. She was grilling steaks and roasting potatoes. He smiled crookedly. There was even corn on there.

"What happened to the kitchen? Did we have a class five hurricane?" The look of pure comical horror from Ryoji made Rachel smile.

"Don't worry. It wasn't a hurricane, and it's not as bad as it looks, " Rachel said, trying to downplay its destruction.

"Have you seen the kitchen?" Ryoji complained, sweeping his hand back to make her take a second look. "It looks like Dante's Inferno in there."

"Since you were doing something nice for me, I wanted to do something nice for you, by having dinner made by the time you got home. I just tried to cook something simple and failed epically. It was only a small grease fire."

"A small grease fire?" He chuckled, and he raised one eyebrow at her.

"I talked to James this afternoon. He's forgiven me and he's going to redo our kitchen."

"Rachel, HOW the hell did you blow up the kitchen?" Ryoji questioned her, once again looking toward the ruined kitchen.

"Well…," Rachel began, stifling the urge to run.

Ryoji was so different now. He made her feel like a kid in trouble with her daddy. How had he changed so much by just putting on a pair of pants? Would she suddenly become demure and sweet if she dared to put on a skirt?

"How can you cook with charcoal and **FIRE**, but you can't master an electric stove?! IT DOESN'T HAVE A FLAME! It's hard to burn yourself with one." Ryoji comically chastised her.

"My people discovered fire. Hence, we are the masters of it. This new-fangled technology confuses me." Rachel smirked as she held her grill tongs like a club and slumped like a Neanderthal.

Ryoji laughed so hard that he had to hold his sides. How Rachel was that? "This is a new year, and by god, you are going to learn to cook. I refuse to have you blow up my kitchen again if I'm working and can't feed you."

"That's why TV dinners were invented. Besides, it's on my to-do list." Rachel turned and tended to the grill. "By the way, that suit looks really good on you."

Ryoji looked down at himself. He really did look amazing in his perfectly tailored suit. He especially looked good because half of it was missing. His tie was hanging loosely around his neck, his shirt was open, revealing his surprisingly toned chest, and he wore it like a tuxedo—with Style.

"Like it?" Ryoji gave her a lopsided grin. "Because you're going to see a lot more of it."

"Really, why is that?" Rachel turned to face him.

Ryoji stiffened, paling at the realization of his slip. He hadn't wanted to break it to Rachel like this. He was supposed to butter her up ... bribe her with spaghetti and bedroom exercise. But he had blown it. Luckily, he was saved when the telephone rang. Rachel stepped inside and answered it.

"Hello. Mr. McPherson? Yes, sir. Hi Frank. He did? You are? Yes, sir. First thing tomorrow morning? Yes, sir." Rachel replied, her voice becoming brighter and brighter with each response.

Rachel hung up. She shook her head, and her mouth dropped open with utter joy and excitement. Then, she clinched her fists and triumphantly pumped the air.

"I LIVE!!" Rachel couldn't contain herself and jumped up and down, almost touching the ceiling each time. "I'M ALIVE. HUH HUH. SO ALIVE!!"

"Good news?" Ryoji asked. He had taken up sitting in a lawn chair to wait for dinner.

Rachel stopped jumping with excitement just long enough to return to the balcony and answer him. "That was Frank. He says that Bishop Able called him. He told him that moderation was a virtue and that liquor was the devil's drink. He's forgiven us for last night's antics and agreed to back my play. He also convinced Frank to forgive Olivia's outbursts, and Frank's giving her a second chance." Rachel leapt into the chair with Ryoji, joyfully. She almost choked him in a fierce hug. "I've been redeemed and I'm back in Frank's good graces. I had better make this perfect. I can't lose this second chance. I am going to tell Mac and James the good news."

"That's good to hear. I'm glad for you." Ryoji smiled brightly. "Bishop Able really isn't a bad guy. He's just staunch in his beliefs."

Rachel looked at Ryoji and ran her fingers through his hair very playfully. "I don't know what you said to him, but thank you. You've saved my life. Hey, wait a minute; you cut your hair. I thought it was just pulled back, but you cut it all off. Why?" Rachel stood and pulled him to stand before her. She moved around him, caressed his hair, and assessed the new Ryoji. "Rollie, your hair…" Rachel moaned with great sadness.

"A new suit, new haircut, and a new me; I doubt the good bishop would've listened to me at all if I had been wearing a dress." Ryoji ran his fingers through his short, spiky hair.

"You sacrificed yourself for me? How could you do that? I know I mean a lot to you, but you didn't have to do that. I bet he made you swear never to wear a dress again and always to wear men's clothes." Rachel said softly, her voice almost in tears at his sacrifice for her.

"Yeah, he did." Ryoji nodded sadly as Rachel looked at him like a completely new person. *She still likes me, right? She isn't thrown by my new haircut or my suit, is she?* "But for you…for you it's no sacrifice at all. I'm still the same Ryoji, dress or no dress." Then he gave her a smile, and his face brightened. "Besides, it's a new year. It's time for a change, isn't it?"

"Ryoji, you are the wind and rain to my dying Earth. I love you more than air. I would marry you tomorrow, if you'd have a nut like me." Rachel told him, as she once again crushed him in a hug.

"I gladly accept," Ryoji said, wrapping his arms around her and returning her affection. It was a soft and sincere mumble meant only for Rachel.

At this, Rachel stepped back and looked at him, blinking. *Is he really saying yes?* She looked up into his eyes and saw his honest sincerity.

"You want to marry me? You seriously want to get married?" *I don't want to sound skeptical, but I just can't imagine it. Ryoji is willing to put up with my madness...my drama...my horrible fashion sense, and my inability to cook.*

"I've always wanted to marry you. I've known that since the day you badgered that banker into giving me a loan for my first store. I need your fire, your strength, and your vibrancy. I don't think I would've gotten this far without you. However, I also know how you feel about marriage. You've always said you'd be a bachelor forever." Ryoji confessed as he looked deep into her eyes. "I remember you said once, 'You know why they call marriage an institution, because you'd have to be crazy to do it'. You said it jokingly, but you weren't. It summed up your feelings about marriage quite well. So, I made myself promise never to ask you or to even bring up the subject, unless you did first."

Rachel smiled as she gently touched Ryoji's face. He knew her so well. He could see through her shell of jokes and snippy comments. He could guess what she was thinking before she even said it. He even knew exactly how she felt whenever she walked through the door. She was crazy...crazy about Ryoji, and crazy people did belong in an institution.

Rachel sighed with purpose and got down on one knee. She took Ryoji's right hand and kissed the back of his hand.

"Sato Ryoji, I love you with all my heart and would be honored if you would consent to be my wife…uh, husband. I am crazy, but I wouldn't want to be institutionalized with anyone but you. Rollie, will you marry me?"

A grin so big crossed Ryoji's face that it actually touched both his ears as he nodded. "Yes. Yes, I will."

"Can I wear one of your dresses? Or should I stick with what I know and wear a tux?" Rachel asked, standing up, her smile matching his.

"Well, if we wed at Bishop Able's church. He will want to see us in "traditional" dress. So, I will design the most beautiful wedding gown in history, just for you." At that moment, Ryo sniffed the air as he sucked in a breath for his next sentence. "What's burning?"

Rachel went from dopey, grinning, and bouncing to paranoid fear and shame. "Oh shit, the steaks!" Rachel rushed away from him, back across the balcony to the grill. Smoke drifted from the charcoal that had once been prime T-bone steaks and the thick, melted lumps that had been potatoes.

"I wonder if James would redo our balcony too," Ryoji giggled at the small fire Rachel was trying to command like her ancestors.

"Stop laughing and get me a fire extinguisher!" She shouted at him.

All of a sudden, the doorbell rang.

"I'll get it," Ryoji called out. He opened the front door and was surprised by who it was. "Hello, Ms. Loy." Ryoji greeted her with a perfect curtsey.

"Ryoji, if you're going to be a gentleman, you'd better learn to bow. Curtseying looks a mite awkward in slacks, you know." Ms. Loy's grin was light and happy.

Ryoji bowed before her, locking his arm in front of his chest and dipping. That was better, a neat, clipped bow. "Sorry, old habits and stuff."

Hearing a voice not Ryoji's and the fire successfully put out, Rachel joined Ryoji in the living room.

"Hello, Rachel. Congratulations." Ms. Loy smiled brightly. "Frank told me that Bishop Able has forgiven you."

"Yes, my man came through for me." Rachel laughed and hugged Ryoji's waist.

Ms. Loy's amused laugh filled the room. It was like a booming bell, light, airy, and full of mirth.

"I also have great news, Ms. Loy," Ryoji announced happily.

"And what is that, a new line of women's wear?" Ms. Loy giggled at him.

"Nope, I'm getting married." He beamed.

"To whom?" Ms. Loy asked, a little more shocked than she meant to be.

"To Rachel." Ryoji hugged Rachel back.

"Really?" Ms. Loy gave them both an amused grin. "Oh, Frank is going to enjoy this. Congratulations, you two."

Ryoji turned to Rachel and asked…

"Did you save dinner?"

"Um…" Rachel blushed and tried to look innocent.

"Ugh, go and see what can be saved, will you?" Ryoji pushed her back towards the balcony. "I need to speak to Ms. Loy for a moment."

"Sure." Rachel laughed as she knelt and pulled cleaning equipment from under the sink. "I just need water and a sponge."

"What?!" Ryoji balked and then sighed heavily. "I guess we're eating out tonight." He chuckled and pinched his nose.

After Rachel left, Ryoji turned to Ms. Loy. She could see his stiffening body, concern and worry written across his face, and furrowed brow.

"You wanted to speak to me?" Ms. Loy asked seriously.

"Yes." Ryoji guided Ms. Loy over to the couch and offered her a seat. "How well do you know Paul?"

"I've only known Paul for seven years." Ms. Loy took the seat offered to her and sat down. "Why?"

"What do you think of him?" Ryoji crossed his arms and thought heavily about what he would say.

"Truthfully, I think he's a creep." Ms. Loy looked down at her feet. "Every time he's around, my hairs stand on end. It's like he's always up to something."

"I think that he murdered Victoria," Ryoji told her point-blank.

"What?!" Ms. Loy exclaimed. Then she gave it some serious thought. Her surprise quickly became concern. "Can you prove it?"

"Maybe. I don't know." Ryoji just shrugged. He looked worried.

"What makes you think so?" Ms. Loy questioned him. She sat forward and waited for his explanation. She sincerely wanted to hear this.

"It's just a hunch. I wasn't even thinking about it, until Rachel said that Paul was now the only heir to Frank's throne. I knew that he sabotaged her New Year's party. So, then I thought, what if he was the one who killed Victoria? The pieces fit, and he has the most to gain."

"I can see your point." Ms. Loy looked up at him. "So, what do you plan to do about it. We can't just accuse him without proof."

"Can you make an anonymous call for me to the police and tell them to look for the car at Paul's parents' house?" Ryoji requested.

"His parents' house?" Ms. Loy thought about what he was saying, but still tried to follow his reasoning.

"Well, he can't drive the car in the city. So, he either dumped it or he's hiding it." Ryoji reasoned, as he stroked his chin and paced the floor. "Someone would have found it by now if it had been dumped."

"Oh, I get it. So, he's hidden it. Cause if he had gotten it repaired, then someone would have put two and two together." Ms. Loy deduced, as she snapped her finger with realization.

Ryoji took Rachel's cellphone from the basket by the coffee table. He looked up Paul's information from her phone and gave it to Ms. Loy. "Paul's parents' house is in the suburbs. The house is 1428 San Francisco Road. Got it? Since they're both dead, he could hide anything there and no one would be the wiser."

"1428 San Francisco Road. I got it. I'll send them there." Ms. Loy nodded as she committed the address to memory. Then she stood, grabbed her coat, and headed for the door.

"Thank you, Ms. Loy. I appreciate your help." Ryoji smiled solemnly at her.

"You didn't tell Rachel of your fears, did you?" Ms. Loy asked, with a knowing grin.

"I tried to. But...she doesn't think he did it. She thinks he is a god on stage, but a puppy in real life." Ryoji just shook his head. "All her life, he came up with the plans, but she was the one to execute them. She just doesn't believe he's capable."

"And we know better, don't we?" Said Ms. Loy as she opened the door.

"I just hope I'm not wrong." Ryoji shrugged. "'Cause knowing Rachel, she'd make him our best man."

"Ugh." Ms. Loy groaned, shook that thought from her head, and headed out. "Don't worry, I'll get the bloodhounds on it."

CHAPTER 18

This wasn't the end of Rachel's problems, because once the newspapers and gossip columns got hold of the story about Rachel's New Year's Eve party, they ran with it. Not only did the media hound her, but the police arrested her on suspicion of being an accomplice to several robberies. Rachel was brought in and sat down in the station waiting room.

It was a beige room with dark brown brick floors and hard plastic blue chairs. There was only one door, and it was trimmed in black. There was one large picture window trimmed in white. However, the window didn't face the street. It faced the interior of the police station. All the cops could see what the perps did in here. A cop marched Rachel in, undid her handcuffs, and sat her down. Then he left. Across the room, she saw James, Alex, and Paul.

"What are you guys in for?" Rachel joked and rubbed her sore wrists.

"Oh, the usual." James winked at her.

"Arrested for being just too damn gorgeous?" Rachel broke out laughing.

"You know it." James laughed too.

"Where's your crossdressing boy toy with the bail money?" Alex taunted her with a smirking grin as he sat forward in his chair and waited for his turn to be questioned.

"At home with the kids." Rachel gave him a wicked grin and blew him a kiss.

"Ugh, you people are crazy," Alex complained, blew them both off, and sat back.

"Rachel, what are we doing here?" Paul asked nervously.

"Well, near as I can tell. James and Alex are accused of theft. I'm accused of aiding and abetting."

"And me?" Paul asked, crossing his arms and sitting back.

"Murder." Rachel stopped smiling and looked at him.

"What?!" Paul jumped up from his seat, fear colored his face, as he looked at Rachel. "Tell me that you're joking."

Rachel sat back, put her hands behind her head, and rocked back and forth in her chair. "Wish I was, but I overheard them talking. Something about your parents' place and a car."

"Shit." Paul bit his thumb and looked away.

"Wait a minute." Rachel stopped rocking her chair and leaned forward. "What are you worried about? You didn't do anything."

"Of course not." Paul bristled, stood, and then started pacing the floor.

"Paul," Rachel called out to him as she stood up. "Look at me. Tell me that you didn't…" Her eyes narrowed on him.

"What?" Paul balked at her and then gave her a dirty look. "Of course not!"

James sat closer to Alex. Alex noticed.

"What are you doing?" Alex asked him, and he pushed James away.

"I've seen that look before. Rachel doesn't believe him. And if Paul is convicted of murder.

She will be too." James warned Alex. "Rachel worshipped Victoria."

Alex just looked at James. He looked scared. Alex turned his attention back to Rachel as she marched across the room and grabbed Paul by his perfectly ironed collar.

"What the hell did you do?" She raged, and she shook him by his collar.

"I did nothing." Paul insisted and pushed her hands away from him.

"Rollie was right. You did do it." Rachel pushed Paul.

"You would listen to that crossdressing calamite and not your best friend since grade school!" Paul shouted at her. "What did sleeping with him rot your brains or something?"

"You leave him out of this!" Rachel shouted right back. "He's a better man than you are!"

"I highly doubt that." Paul scoffed and brushed her off.

"So where were you that night?" Rachel glared at Paul.

"At home, sleeping," Paul told her as he faced off against her. "Where were you? On your knees, no doubt. That's the only way that you or Victoria could beat me."

The strike came so fast that nobody saw it coming. James and Alex both flinched as they saw Rachel's right fist punch Paul so hard that she dropped him to the floor in one punch.

"You son of a bitch." Rachel raged, as she stood over Paul, both her fists balled up and ready to fight. "You did do it. Why?! WHY WOULD YOU DO THAT?!" Rachel dropped her knee on his stomach and held him there as she punched him over and over in the face.

"Get off me, you rabbit dog!" Paul flung punches of his own and tried to push her off him.

Suddenly, the door burst open, and two cops rushed in, followed by Mr. McPherson and Ryoji. The cops grabbed Rachel by her waist and pulled her off Paul. Both of them were still shouting and screaming obscenities at each other. James noticed that Paul looked like a raccoon and that Rachel looked like a Dalmatian.

"Can we be moved to a quieter holding cell?" James joked.

"Rachel, stop it! Stop!" Ryoji ran over to her and tried to calm her down. He grabbed Rachel's chin and forced her to look at him. "Rachel, stop." He demanded.

Rachel snorted angrily, stopped fighting the two cops, and started pacing in her corner. Mr. McPherson went to check on Paul.

"What did ye do this time?" Mr. McPherson chuckled as he picked Paul up off the floor.

"Me?!" Paul yelled at Mr. McPherson. "This isn't my fault. Why don't you ask her why she's been arrested?"

"I know why she's here." Mr. McPherson laughed. "Who do ye think Ryoji asked tae bail her out?"

"Typical," Paul growled as he pulled away from Mr. McPherson.

"Why don't ye tell me why yer bail is way higher than hers?" Mr. McPherson requested of Paul calmly.

Paul said nothing at first. "I have no idea." He lied. He crossed his arms and turned away from Mr. McPherson.

"Then I'll tell ye." Mr. McPherson said. "They have ye here fur the murder of Victoria Cross."

"I didn't do it." Paul uncrossed his arms, snarled, and looked Mr. McPherson right in the eye. "Why don't you believe me?"

"Actually, I do." Said Mr. McPherson. "That's why I've secured the best lawyers for ye."

"You shouldn't waste the money," Rachel growled at Mr. McPherson.

Mr. McPherson just chuckled at her. "Ryoji, why don't ye take yer little tigress and git some ice for her eye."

"Yes, sir." Ryoji put an arm around Rachel and guided her to the door. "Come on, dear, let's get you checked out of this institution." He chuckled.

"And Rachel," Mr. McPherson called out to her.

"Yes, sir," Rachel stopped walking and gave Mr. McPherson her attention.

"I want tae see ye in mah office tomorrow." He narrowed his eyes on her. "Cause I don't make enough money tae keep ye and Paul out of jail, if this is going tae become a thing with ye two."

"But I…" Rachel began. She clinched her fists, but then stopped, and took a deep breath. "Yes, sir."

"Come on, Rocky." Ryoji chuckled. "I'll get you some ice for your eye and ice cream for your tummy."

Rachel noticed that Ryoji wore designer blue jeans and a white polo shirt. "You look good."

"Ha-ha-ha, and you look like Spuds Mackenzie." Ryoji laughed as he walked his fiancée out the door.

"As for ye Paul, ye and I are going tae talk as well." Mr. McPherson told Paul. "But fur now, ye're going tae talk tae mah lawyer."

"This way, Mr. Cartwright." One of the cops gestured for him to follow.

Paul clicked his tongue and glared at the cop, but followed him anyway.

"What about us?" James asked.

Mr. McPherson looked at James and his partner, Alex.

"I don't know ye boys well enough tae stick mah neck out for ye." Mr. McPherson told them point-blank, as he stood in front of them.

"Fair enough." James sighed heavily.

"But." Mr. McPherson said, and he too gave a reluctant sigh. "Rachel trusted ye two enough tae hire ye. So, I will give ye the benefit of the doubt. Therefore, I have secured lawyers for ye as well."

Both James and Alex brightened up and sat up straight.

"Thank you, Mr. McPherson." James gushed happily.

"Yeah, Thanks." Alex gave a small grin and ran his fingers through his hair.

"But," Mr. McPherson glared angrily at both of them. "If either of ye get mah girl into any more trouble."

"I won't," promised James. "I promise."

"Don't worry." Alex blew him off as he looked at James. "Our association is at an end."

"Good." Mr. McPherson's face and mood lightened. "Officer, I believe that their lawyers are waiting fur them."

"Come on, you two." The cop ordered with a snarl. "Let's get moving."

Chapter 19

It was bad enough that the papers saw Rachel as bisexual, but now she was also seen as a small-time criminal. Frank had no choice but to start working on damage control. If she wanted to keep her backers, Ryoji and Rachel had to start acting like normal people.

So, Frank was forcing Rachel and Ryoji to go out on a real date. He had announced their engagement to the world to stave off the backlash that would happen when the world found out that the famous Sato Ryoko was really a Sato Ryoji. However, Frank had the whole thing planned out. Rachel and Ryoji would go to dinner, and then dancing, and then they could do whatever they wanted as long as they did it like a real boy and a real girl.

As time was ticking away, Rachel felt more and more stupid. Even though she was wearing one of Ryoji's designer dresses and looked stunning, she felt awkward, bare, and almost naked. She tugged at the thin material.

"Rollie! Did you have to make the dress so thin?" Rachel pulled at the dress as she looked down at it.

Rachel felt like the very air was brushing against her skin. The dress's material felt too close to her skin and moved in strange ways. It was a black sleeveless evening dress with a floral print in gold, a high circular neckline, and a fitted body waist that fitted to the knees and was paneled straight to the floor where it flared out into a mermaid hem.

However, Rachel's worst complaint about this dress was that it was backless. The air around her seemed to caress and tickle her. Ryoji sighed with pride as he added the last finishing touches. The dress was beautiful on her. The thin satin shine made her skin glow, and the tapered waist gave Rachel more curves than a mountain pass.

"You look amazing, Rachel. Do you know how long I've wanted to put you in a dress?" he smirked. "Just relax."

He had shoved his fiancée into a sleeveless dress because it was elegant and beautiful, and because Rachel's karate lessons had given her a wonderfully toned body. Unfortunately, two things were going against him there. One, trying to get Rachel to shave her arms had been a nightmare. In the end, he ended up doing it for her after having tied her to the bed. Two, Rachel was really strong. More than once, she had hip-tossed him to the floor to get out of doing this. But Frank insisted, and Ryoji knew how to press her buttons.

"Rollie, I feel stupid. Dresses are your thing," Rachel whined. She scratched her arms, feeling the bumps rising. "You know this would not have been necessary if you had just let me wear a suit. I know I'm a girl, but girls in suits are sexy!"

Ryoji ignored her comment and adjusted his tie...again. Why anyone would willingly hang themselves with one of these things was beyond him.

"Women in suits, huh? Think about it, if you think you feel stupid, then imagine how I feel. I feel like I'm choking to death in a straitjacket. It's a tailored suit and I feel...confined." With that, Ryoji yanked off the tie and merely opened the top two buttons of his shirt. *Might as well go with a more debonair look.*

"See! We should stay here, just you and me. I'll even let you tie me to the bed again, if you'd just forget the entire damned date. I don't want to trudge around with the whole city looking through my clothes, and my back is freezing. Why are we even doing this again?" Rachel grumbled, complained, and continued to scrabble at the dress, which she felt was not covering nearly enough of her body.

Ryoji smacked her hands away from her arms and hissed at her, "Stop it, and be a lady, Rachel. If I can handle it, so can you." Ryoji tittered irritably and chewed his lips, his eyes fluttered in a very pretty and hypnotic way to draw attention to them. He licked his lips, confused by the lack of flavored lip gloss, and pouted.

"Ryoji, you're being a girl again." Rachel corrected him, and she sighed heavily. She was completely against going out tonight. "Now,

Dinner...me in a gown...you not wearing pink panties... us, why?" Rachel looked at Ryoji and envied his suit. "Why don't you switch clothes with me? Please."

Ryoji's eyes widened, and he stopped. "Because that would defeat the purpose of tonight." He sighed and swept his hair back. "We're doing this to show the tabloids that you are dating a man. That last article after the party was really scathing. And that picture of us kissing didn't help one bit. People are afraid that your sexuality will bleed into the plays. Frank calls this damage control. Not to mention your jail time." He quipped.

"Frankly my dear, I don't give a damn." Rachel giggled with her best Clark Gable accent.

"I know you don't, and it shouldn't matter, but to normal people it does."

Ryoji adjusted Rachel's dress, smoothing it out a little. Then he slid around her in a strangely graceful swish of his hips, wrapping a string of pearls around her neck. He almost forgot that he wasn't dressing one of his dummies but his fiancée.

"What the hell?" Rachel gawked at the lovely string of gorgeous pearls.

"Oh, shut up. They complement the dress." Ryoji gently placed them on her and leaned in to fasten the clasp. "A lady must have the perfect accessories."

"Yeah, you would know, Ryoji. Fine, but I'm not carrying that tiny ass handbag. Just what do they expect girls to put into those tiny things anyway? My wallet won't even fit in there. I guess the mystery is solved about why girls never pay for dinner."

"Rachel, so help me if you don't stop complaining..." Ryoji scolded her, placing his hands on his hips.

"You'll what?" Rachel stared him down playfully and tugged on the edges of his jacket. "Tie me down again. Go ahead. I'd enjoy that more than being paraded like a spectacle in this get-up. My hair has swirls in places where they do not belong. So exactly what would you do to me, my little lady?"

That's when Ryoji got really wicked ideas. He rubbed his chin and licked his lips. He cocked his hips with his hands on it and said, "Well, I could start with a spanking."

"Ooh, that doesn't sound like a reason to stop complaining to me," Rachel grinned. She kissed Ryoji, pulled him closer to her, and then boldly squeezed his buttocks. "Sounds more like a reason to stay home to me."

Ryoji gasped at Rachel's groping, but then smiled, and deepened the kiss. They were utterly lost in each other's arms, but just then the clock chimed the hour. Ryoji stopped kissing her and gently pushed her away. "A lady is never late."

"Oh, please. It takes them three hours to dress." Rachel snorted. " That's why the phrase "fashionably late" was invented."

"Maybe, but..." began Ryoji, but he didn't finish as Rachel dove in for another kiss. Ryoji's eyes fell shut as Rachel enticed his tongue to dance with hers, and he felt as if she was pulling his very breath from him. Suddenly, he remembered that they were supposed to be leaving. He summoned his resolve and pushed her away. "Rachel, stop. We have to go."

"Ugh, you and your damn reason, Rollie. I was trying to distract you."

"And doing a damn good job," Ryoji chuckled at her. "but if we don't hurry, we'll miss our seating and then Frank will be mad again."

"If it were anyone else but Frank," Rachel groaned. She tugged at her dress one last time and felt her feet aching from the three-inch heels.

"I know. You'd skip it. But you can't, so come on." Ryoji urged her as he helped her into her coat.

Later, at Dekota's Restaurant, Ryoji and Rachel arrived just in time to be seated.

"Now remember, Rachel, no fidgeting, no biting your nails, and no eating like a Neanderthal." Ryoji ticked each of his words off on a carefully maintained, but unpainted fingers.

"Me?" Rachel quipped, in mock hurt and embarrassment. "Just you remember, no hand movements, no twirling your hair, no crossing your legs, and none of that swishing. Of course, if we had stayed home, you could've swished all you want."

"Oh, this is going to be one hell of an evening." Ryoji sighed, glancing at his brand-new gold men's wristwatch.

"Name, please," The Head Waiter ordered. He raised an eyebrow at the big woman tapping her foot and cursing under her breath, as the breeze from the door ruffled her hair. She crossed her arms and chewed her lips irritably as Ryoji stood there. The stewardess took their coats and gave them a ticket stub.

"We're the Sato Party," Rachel announced boldly. It was only natural for her to say who they were. Ryoji never took the lead.

"Ah, yes, Mr. and Mrs. Sato. Follow me, please, " the waiter requested. He showed them to their table. Ryoji swayed irritably, his hips swaying gently as he followed the host.

"We're married already, are we?" Rachel whispered to Ryoji. "That's still another month off."

"We're betrothed. It's the same thing. Just haven't walked down the aisle yet. Technically," Ryoji tittered, as he followed Rachel, "We've lived together for years. Common Law marriage and whatnot."

Ryoji followed the headwaiter into the seating area with Rachel on his arm. The headwaiter stopped at a table in the middle of the room.

"Ah, couldn't we have a table in the corner?" Rachel asked, barely refraining from covering her wide rear end from the stares people were giving it. She shot Ryoji a hateful look for the dress again and pleaded with the host.

"Mr. McPherson said to give you our best table," the host said, snapping his fingers and causing several waiters to appear. Enjoy your evening."

"Oh boy," Rachel sighed, and pinched the bridge of her nose.

The other waiters started staring at each other as Ryoji and Rachel stood there. Ryoji was a little curious as to why Rachel was just standing there. She was definitely trying to signal something to him with her eyes, but what? That's when he remembered. Rachel always pulled his chair out for him, but now, it was his turn. He was the guy tonight. *God, this is going to be a long night.*

"Oh, sorry, Rachel, I spaced there for a minute." He pulled out her chair for her and stifled the urge to twirl his finger in his hair.

"Just pretend you're me." Rachel chuckled as she sat down and placed the folded napkin in her lap.

"Does that include making passes at the waitresses?" Ryoji snickered as he too sat down.

"Hey, whatever floats your boat." She told Ryoji. Then she leered at one of the waitresses as she pushed a dessert cart to the next table. "They are wearing very well-fitted skirts."

"Rachel!" Ryoji warned, as one of his eyebrows began to quiver with annoyance.

"Sorry, love. Bad habit." Rachel smiled apologetically. "You're the only guy for me. And you know that." She winked at him playfully.

Now that the two were seated, the waiters began setting up the table for two and brought wine and breadsticks for them. Ryoji and Rachel took some time looking over the menu. There was just so much to choose from.

"Well, what do you feel like tonight?" Ryoji asked simply. He lifted his glass and took a drink of water.

"I feel like an idiot on parade," Rachel grumbled, as she mindlessly pulled at the string of pearls around her neck. They were irritating and, like the dress, felt unnatural to her. "Why do women have to adorn themselves like Christmas trees?"

"Stop that," Ryoji squealed. His big green eyes got watery, and he batted Rachel's hands away from the necklace. Then he scowled at her like an angry girl who had lost her favorite shoes. "You might break them. Those are my best pearls, and you know very well that I meant dinner."

"Meat and potatoes, Ryoji, you know that. I am a Neanderthal, remember?" She quipped as she tilted her head to the right.

"Oh, come on, broaden your horizons a little. Why not try the Grilled Texas Quail with lime bean relish, sweet port sauce, and prosciutto chips? They also have Pan-Seared half-Maine lobster with Baby arugula, which is very low in calories. Arugula is very good for you, too. You can get that with pickled red onions, hazelnuts, and a chardonnay herb dressing."

"Ryoji, men do not worry about calories. They don't have to worry about their girlish figures." Rachel leaned back, her knees spread, and laughed at Ryoji's expression.

"Oh god, you're horrible. Women don't sit like football players when wearing a dress." Ryoji kicked her chair and forced it back onto all fours.

"I'm not horrible," Rachel said, carefully crossing her legs to stop flashing the other side of the restaurant. "I'm simple."

"I'm leaving that one alone." He laughed.

"You always were the smart one." Rachel took one last look at the menu before she gave up completely. "Ok, how about the Scottish Seafood in honor of Frank?"

"I think I'll have the Australian Lobster tails." Ryoji took both menus and handed them back to the waiter.

"Ok, that's dinner," Rachel said, pushing a wayward strand of her hair back and out of her face.

The waiter left to place their order, leaving them alone to talk and drink their wine. Rachel took a sip and then thought it better not to drink tonight, so she pushed her glass away from her.

"You don't like it?" Ryoji asked, tasting his wine.

"No, it's fine." Rachel sighed. "It's just that drinking got me into this mess."

"Quite right," Ryoji chuckled, and he too placed his glass far away from him. "It's good to see that you do learn from your mistakes."

"So, what shall we do after dinner?" Rachel asked, looking at the pristine table setting and then at the restaurant's lush and lavish decor. God, this place is swank."

"Ha-ha-ha, why are you so uncomfortable in places such as this?" He asked as he watched her look around.

"Because I grew up in a house that had nothing breakable in it for a reason." She told him honestly, with a slight grin, as she remembered her childhood.

"We are so made for each other, you and me. I grew up in a house where everything was breakable." He smiled, but then his smile turned into a frown as he remembered. "Even the people in it."

Rachel just watched him as he thought back on sadder times. She also watched him begin to twirl his very short hair. He always did that when he was nervous or upset. Rachel cleared her throat.

"Ryoji, hair." That was all she had to say. Ryoji immediately stopped the nervous habit and placed his hands in his lap. Thankfully, the salads arrived. Now giving his hands something to do, he elegantly ate his salad. Rachel just watched him. "Do guys eat their salads like that?"

"What do you want me to do?" He whispered harshly, with a mocking grin. "Use my fingers like you do?"

"Why not?" Rachel asked nonchalantly as she picked up a fork.

"Not bloody likely. I don't think there are any finger foods on this menu."

"That's what this place is missing." Rachel beamed. "Spicy Buffalo Wings and a good beer." Rachel licked her lips and then gave the bottle of wine a hateful glare. She seemed to be trying to will it to become a bottle of her favorite malt.

Ryoji cheered up. "Uh, yeah, I don't think so. Society isn't ready for your poor eating habits." Rachel just looked at her salad and then made a face. Ryoji noticed. "They're vegetables, Rach. Just eat them."

"I don't want to." She pouted and crossed her arms.

"Don't you want to grow up to be a beautiful girl...like me?" Ryoji let his face soften, and Rachel gawked at how he instantly took on a feminine appearance even in his tailored suit. He batted his eyes and giggled, and Rachel was almost jealous of how pretty he still was. Rachel smiled, and Ryoji laughed. He noticed how Rachel ate her salad. "Not so much at one time. Take a little bit like this."

"No wonder you're so skinny." She covered her mouth as she spoke with a mouth full of salad. "I'll starve to death eating like that."

"I'll make a woman out of you yet." He handed her a napkin. "That I swear."

"I'll become a woman, the day I see you scratch your crotch and spit."

"Ugh, Rachel, don't be vulgar; gentlemen, do not scratch and spit." Ryoji grimaced. "Besides... sit up straight...have I told you how elegant you look?" He smiled softly at her, and his eyes twinkled.

"Humph, yeah right." Rachel scoffed and rolled her eyes at him.

Ryoji smiled as he looked at Rachel. Though she tried to deny it as much as she could, Rachel

Washington was not an ugly girl. True, she wasn't a stunning beauty, but that was not why Ryoji had fallen in love with her in the first place. She had a quiet power about her, which was her self-confidence, and it got louder the more she talked.

But tonight, in a dress, Rachel was the most vulnerable that Ryoji had ever seen her. He had done her hair up to show off the necklace, but the aura of chic that the classic black dress that matched her hair gave her was spellbinding. Ryoji smiled. He loved her so much that he wanted this to work with all his heart. But wishing for it to happen wouldn't help. He had to become a knight, and she had to become a lady, just like in the stories that Rachel loved so much.

"Rachel," Ryoji called to her.

"Hm," Rachel replied, mindlessly pushing her salad around with her fork.

"Let's play a game." He offered, as he straightened his chair, sat up straight, and brushed back his hair.

"A game?" Rachel questioned him as she took a sip of her water.

"Yes. You pretend to be a lady, and I will pretend to be your knight."

Rachel considered this. *Yes, why not? This was a game, after all, a game to fool the press*. She smiled at him and nodded. "Sure, I'll play. What are the rules?"

"The Rules of Society."

"Oh, bloody hell." Rachel's shoulders dropped decidedly.

"No swearing." He mocked her as he shook a warning finger at her.

"This is gonna be a hard game." Rachel shook her head and pinched the bridge of her nose. Now wishing that she hadn't agreed so readily.

"And use proper English." He chuckled deliciously.

"On second thought, I don't wanna play."

"That's three for me." He kept grinning at her. "Are you just going to quit without a fight?"

Rachel smirked at him. "What do I get if I win?"

"Me," Ryoji said, taking another bite of his salad.

Rachel raised an eager eyebrow, thinking of everything she would love for Ryoji to do. A wicked grin spread across her face. "And if I lose."

"Another dress."

"Ugh..." Rachel growled at the thought of another dress. But then if she won, she wouldn't have to wear it. "You're on."

"Good. From now on, we are Lord and Lady Sato from the land of Sword and Might." Ryoji lifted his glass of water and took a sip.

"Hahaha, can I be a ninja?" She asked, her eyes shining with delight.

Ryoji blanched and nearly spat his water onto the table. But he held his composure, wiped his mouth with his napkin, and then, with an amused grin, said, "No."

And just like that, their dinner arrived. A camera flashed from a table near the kitchen, while the other reporter took notes.

"So, Rachel Washington is having dinner with her future husband, Sato Ryoji. How boring?" The reporter commented to her cameraman.

"True, they were more fun as cross-dressers." He laughed, taking another picture of Ryoji as he twirled his hair.

"Still, Rachel Washington marrying Sato Ryoko, now that is news." The reporter plotted, adding her own spin to the story.

"You are devious." The cameraman praised his partner.

"Thank you. It's a living." The reporter smiled. "Good news is always interesting."

After dinner, Rachel and Ryoji decided to go and see a play. Twelfth Night, Rachel's favorite play, was being performed tonight. Since it was a lovely night, they decided to walk to the theater.

"Are they still behind us?" Rachel asked. She stopped again, as her heels were really beginning to hurt her feet.

"Yes," Ryoji told her, barely looking back.

"Geez, I'm going to break an ankle in these things." She griped as she used Ryoji to steady herself.

"Quite frankly, I'm surprised you lasted this long in them." Ryoji quipped as he pulled Rachel closer to him for support.

"You are so lucky that I know karate and have an excellent sense of balance."

"Yes, yes, I am," chuckled Ryoji. "I can only imagine what the papers would say tomorrow if you had fallen in them."

Rachel just punched his arm.

"No violence." Ryoji reminded her.

"Yeah," agreed a rough and garish voice. "Listen to your boyfriend."

Rachel and Ryoji looked to their left and saw a man in his thirties pointing a gun at them. Rachel didn't even think about it; she just moved into action. She grabbed his gun hand, pointed it out and away from Ryoji, and tried to knee the guy in the head as she brought his head down, but the dress she was wearing restricted her movements.

"What the hell?!" Rachel swore as she realized that this was not going to work. "Damn this dress."

With her distracted, the thug hit her with a hard left and pushed her away. Rachel tripped in her heels and twisted her ankle. She fell to the ground, and before she could get up, she was looking down the barrel of a gun.

"Bad move, lady." He laughed as he got ready to pull the trigger.

Suddenly, out of nowhere, the thug was kicked in the face, and he fell to the ground. Surprised by the blow, he dropped the gun. Rachel had been stunned that she couldn't fight, angry that this thug had bested her, and shamed at being helpless. But all that disappeared as she watched Ryoji jump into action.

"Holy shyte." She gaped as Ryoji tossed his dinner jacket to her. Rachel put the jacket on so it wouldn't touch the ground, then returned her attention to her fiancée. He was being incredibly cool. "Oh, Ryoji, go, boy, go."

Ryoji finished the guy off with a hard right punch and knocked him out. But that was not to be the end of it. Five more guys came out of the shadows.

"Lookie here, fellas, we got ourselves a kung fu hero," laughed one.

"Oh yeah, it's time for some fun. We'll beat him down and take his girl, one by one," laughed another.

Take Rachel from him? As the image of these five men dishonoring his wife-to-be rolled around in his head, Rachel saw something she had never seen before. Ryoji usually had a submissive nature, but now he was mad, and all that submission disappeared in the hellish red glow of his anger.

"The hell you will. Rachel is mine. She belongs to me and only me."

"Not for long," laughed the one in a muddy blue shirt. "Kill him."

With that, all five attacked him at once. Rachel could only watch, stunned and full of pride, as her man laid down one royal beatdown. Ryoji waited until they were all within kicking distance, and that's when he unleashed his roundhouse right kick. That knocked them all out, but they were not that easily defeated. They got back up, and Ryoji went to work on them. One tried to punch him, but he blocked that punch and kicked him in the face with his knee. Rachel had tried to do the same move in the dress but couldn't. The man fell back and hit his head on the curb. He was out and would have a very nasty headache tomorrow.

Another tied to grab Ryoji from behind. Ryoji let him go and then threw his head back, breaking the guy's nose. As he let Ryoji go, Ryoji turned and kicked him in his left leg hard. Even Rachel winced when she heard the crack of breaking bones. Another tried to knife Ryoji, but he grabbed the man's knife hand, twisted his wrist, and bent it up. The man howled in pain and dropped the knife. Then Ryoji twisted his arm again and dislocated it for good measure. He bawled like a baby as his arm just dangled there. That was it for him; he ran away.

The other two knew karate or thought they did. They fired punches and kicks at Ryoji, hoping to catch him off guard and overpower him. However, Ryoji's skill was much higher than theirs. He blocked their punches and kicks and backed up each time. To an observer, it would look like Ryoji was losing, but to Rachel's trained eye, he was waiting for an opening. It came when both men started getting tired. Ryoji struck so fast that if Rachel had blinked, she would have missed it.

Ryoji hit one in the throat, and as he backed up choking, Ryoji turned and hit the other one with a very hard left-handed punch, which he finished with a forward kick that sent the guy flying into the alley. The choking one had seen what Ryoji had done to his friend and decided he had had enough. He motioned for no more and ran away into the night. Ryoji watched him leave, and then he looked down in contempt at the three unconscious ones. He smoothed out his hair, and then he went to check on Rachel.

"Are you alright?" He asked her as he looked over her sprained ankle.

"I'm...I'm..." Rachel looked at him with stars in her eyes.

"Did they hurt you?" He questioned and helped her to stand up.

"I'm speechless and frigging proud of my boy. Where did you learn to fight like that?" gushed Rachel, as she favored her right foot and placed her weight on the left foot.

"Sometimes you forget that I wasn't always a girl. I studied martial arts in Japan. Besides, you don't think I took you to all your lessons and didn't pick up anything."

"Ryoji," Rachel gasped, still in awe of that incredible fight. "Today, you are a man."

Ryoji just laughed as he picked Rachel up in his arms. "You do know that you just lost our game. First of all, for fighting and second of all, for your foul language."

"So be it. I deserve it for having to be saved." Rachel frowned. "I hate being helpless."

"I'm just glad you're OK." Ryoji leaned his forehead to hers.

Rachel lay her head upon his chest. "I'm more than OK," she purred, enjoying the warmth of his body. Then, a chilling reality brought her back to the present. "Uhm, Ryoji."

"Yes." He answered her, as he effortlessly bridal carried her.

"You're not going to carry me all the way home like this, are you?"

"Why? Is it too embarrassing for your **manhood** if I carry you like a girl?"

"Well, I do have a reputation to uphold." She grinned. "But no, I just don't want you wearing yourself out before we get home."

Ryoji just laughed at her. "Hahaha, well then, I'll just have to show you how strong I really am."

Not far away, the camera continued flashing.

"Please tell me you got all that! " the reporter exclaimed excitedly, her heart still beating fast.

"Every move. Who knew he could fight so well?" laughed the cameraman. "It still would have been funnier to watch him do it in heels."

The reporter giggled. "True, that would have been too good."

"So, are you going to write an honest report?"

"Yes, I am. I feel these two will have a true life much stranger than fiction."

CHAPTER 20

"Ladies and Gentlemen, we are gathered here today to join this man and this woman in holy matrimony." Bishop Able announced grandly.

He stared out at the congregation and nodded. His smile was heavy and respectful, but it was indescribable joy. He loved weddings. Not only was his church gaily decorated in blush pink, ivory, and gold, but the glorious morning sun shone through the stained-glass windows and bathed the church in radiant light. It did his heart good to join two people in love and ask God to bless them.

"By the way, that is a lovely dress," The bishop complimented Rachel.

"Think so?" Rachel squeezed Ryoji's hand as the bishop nodded again. "My husband-to-be designed it for me."

"You're a good **man**, Ryoji."

Ryoji beamed at the compliment. He was a good man, and Rachel was a good woman. They just weren't what you would call a traditional couple, but they were perfect for each other. Sarah and Mac sat together arm in arm in the first pew on the bride's side of the aisle.

"I'm a good man, too." Mac whispered to Sarah, sliding a small velvet box into her hand.

"What is this?"

It seemed that the bishop wasn't the only one who enjoyed whispering during important ceremonies. It was a family tradition, down to his daughter.

"Don't open it until after the service." Mac's grin was full of mystery and just around the edges, love. It softened him, made him more normal, and gave his smile a light hint of lust.

Sarah dropped the box into her purse, sitting beside her. "Mackenzie Eubank, you're a tease." She gently elbowed his ribs as she leaned against him.

"Don't you ever forget it," Mac whispered, giving her a peck on the cheek.

"Do you, Sato Ryoji, take this woman to be your lawfully wedded wife?" The question was heavy and felt like it could change the very universe depending on his answer. Ryoji took one look at Rachel and knew his answer was yes. The bishop continued, "To have and to hold from this day forward, for better, for worse, for richer, for poorer, in sickness and health, to love and cherish always."

"I do."

Those two words made Rachel want to swoon and faint like a little prissy lady. *How could two little words that most people say every day feel so powerful right now? It's unnatural. Love really is making me crazy, just like Mac. I feel hot, like I'm burning up, yet I'm shivering with cold. Look at me, my arms were covered in goose bumps.*

"And do you, Rachel Isabella Washington, take this man to be your lawfully wedded husband? In good times and in bad, in sickness and health; to love, honor, and cherish all the days of your lives."

Rachel didn't even have to think. It was the easiest question in the world. It was like asking her what her name was. It was something she just knew by heart. It was the right answer, and she'd never forget the moment when she signed her entrance slip into her new institution.

"I do."

"The rings, please," The Bishop stated, smiling as he nodded to the ring bearer. "I bless these rings with them do thee wed. The ring is a circle, a never-ending loop like your lives will be, forever intertwined and never-ending like love is meant to be."

Ryo placed his ring on Rachel's finger, and Rachel placed her ring on Ryo's finger.

"And so, by the power vested in me…" began the Bishop.

"You're not going to ask if anyone objects?" Rachel snickered.

"Do you really want to give anyone the chance?" The Bishop laughed, and so did Rachel and Ryo. They loved laughter and were rarely serious, so why should their wedding be somber and starkly traditional? "I now pronounce you man and wife. You may kiss the bride."

Ryoji gladly kissed Rachel, and Sarah pecked Mac on the cheek. The bishop glared at Mac while James and his cat both cried.

"Mr. Tabby, we're losing all our friends. I'm always the best man but never the groom." James pouted dramatically as he clapped Ryoji on the shoulder.

"I can't believe you made the cat a best man too," Bishop Able said, groaning.

Mr. Tabby, in an adorable mini-tuxedo, sat at James' feet. He was perfectly behaved and even seemed to bow his head as the entire chapel stood.

"It was the only way to get James to show up." Rachel laughed, staring down at James' cat.

"I've never seen a cat in a tux before." The Bishop commented, shaking his head. "He is well behaved, though."

"Well, we were gonna leave him in just boots, but he still looked naked." Rachel jested as she playfully poked Ryoji in the ribs.

"So, Rachel and James begged me to design it a tux," Ryoji said, finishing Rachel's sentence. "I can't believe I designed a one-of-a-kind tux…for a cat."

"You people need help," Bishop Able said, but his smile gave it away as a mere jest. He really was happy for the oddball group of theatre folk.

After the ceremony, the newlyweds, the Bishop, and everyone else in the sanctuary started to walk out of the church's front doors. All except for Sarah and Mac, who stood in the aisle next to the pew where they had been seated. Sarah looked at Mac.

"Okay, Mac, the service is over." Sarah began, her curiosity making her fingers itch to open the box. What could it be? Earrings? A pendant? A Pin? Every possible outcome, but the obvious ran through her mind.

Mac smiled at her. "Okay, Beautiful, go ahead and open it."

Sarah pulled the box out of her purse and opened it. Right there was the most dazzling diamond ring she'd ever seen. It sparkled and gleamed, and she'd never seen a gem cut to look like a musical note—a beautiful single note.

"OH, MY GOODNESS MAC!!"

Sarah's eyes watered, her throat tightened, and her heart soared to heaven. She cried with joy, bawling and burying her face in his shoulder. She couldn't contain her emotions. Her mother had always said she wore her feelings on her sleeves for everyone to see.

Startled by her outburst, the Bishop turned around to behold Sarah. She was holding the small box, crying, and clutching at Mac's shirt. He glowered at Mac.

"What's wrong, baby girl?" The Bishop asked, very concerned that Mac had broken her heart already.

"Not a thing, Daddy," Sarah replied. She sniffed and took her face from Mac's shoulder to face her father. "Not a thing. It ain't a thing, but a diamond ring." Sarah beamed and held the ring out for her father to see. Her eyes sparkled brighter than they ever had in her life.

The Bishop examined the ring. Well, the rogue had good taste. That ring wasn't cheap, but at least he had the means to take care of his baby girl. Then, the Bishop looked at his daughter's face. Her heart wasn't broken; it was soaring to the moon. His glare softened, and he smiled at her. Then he turned to his wife Mary and assured her that everything was fine, that Sarah and Mac would follow behind them later.

Sarah pulled the ring out of its box. It was a large, sparkling diamond cut like a musical note, with tiny blue stones surrounding its edges. Mac took it from her hand.

"Do you like it, Sarah?" Mac asked, sliding the ring onto her finger. It was a perfect fit, and its ***rightness*** seemed to melt into her skin. "I thought it was only fitting for a muse to be adorned with notes."

Sarah was so overcome by emotion that she couldn't speak. So, she just hugged Mac for all he was worth.

CHAPTER 21

Rachel couldn't help but smile. James had outdone himself with the reception hall. The entrance was a dark tunnel, backlit with pictures of Ryoji and Rachel in various stages of their lives. It was like a living wall of memories. Following the white Christmas lights as they led further in, you were greeted by the tunnel's opening into a great hall. Both Rachel and Ryoji's eyes grew wide with excitement as a wonderland of fantasy and a 1920s speakeasy opened up in front of them.

"What do you know?" Rachel laughed with ecstatic mirth. "James created a speakeasy for wood elves and dwarves."

"Your little buddy really outdid himself." Ryoji praised the decorations, and he escorted Rachel to the affair.

"What the hell," Mackenzie looked around in stunned awe. "James, what did you do?"

"Oh, you know." James smiled brightly. "Given Ryoji's Asian background and Rachel's affinity for fairy tales, I created an Asian speakeasy for fairy tale creatures."

"What on earth?" Bishop Able's mouth fell open in utter surprise.

His wife, Mary, and other members and guests of his church squealed with glee. The bright and playful colors entranced them.

"So, what do ye think?" Mr. McPherson chuckled with a hearty laugh.

"Frank, where do I begin?" Bishop Able kept looking around the room as his wife and her friends gleefully enjoyed the room and its decorations.

Tables lined the room, a large dancefloor in the center, a fully staffed bar on the right side, and a full chef's kitchen on the left churning out dish after dish of succulently delightful temptations for your palate. People cheerfully entered the room, allowing the fantastical atmosphere to transport them to another world. They ate, they sang, and they danced.

As the newlyweds danced, Mr. McPherson and Ms. Loy sat next to Bishop Able and his wife at the main table. Ms. Loy picked up Mr. McPherson's champagne and sipped it. Mr. McPherson hated champagne; he wasn't going to finish it. Mr. McPherson grinned at his lady-friend and nodded at her with smiling eyes. Then, as he looked back up, he saw the Bishop's questioning look.

"What's wrong, Steven?" Mr. McPherson asked, with a deep chuckle.

"Why don't you marry her?" Bishop Able suggested to his best friend with a knowing grin.

"What and ruin a perfectly good secretary?" Mr. McPherson laughed.

Bishop Able just shook his head and pinched the bridge of his nose as he chuckled with mirth. Then he turned his attention back to Rachel and Ryoji.

"It still looks wrong. Both are dressed as they should be, and the picture still looks wrong. What is it about those two that is so strange?" The Bishop wondered.

Mr. McPherson looked at Rachel and Ryoji. They swirled and twirled in perfect rhythm; Rachel's every footstep pulling Ryoji's with it. She set the tempo, and he followed, melding back into their natural flow.

"That's because she's leading," Mr. McPherson said. He pointed to their feet with a fork full of chocolate cake. Unfortunately, he also dangled the cake right in front of Ms. Loy. She pulled the fork to her and snagged his cake.

"You can take the girl out of the country, but you can't take the country out of the girl, I suppose," Bishop Able chuckled, shaking his head.

"Rachel's her own country." Frank snickered, slapping Ms. Loy's hand away from his chicken. "With her own rules and allegiances. She has her own borders and her own customs ... and we don't have passports. Mandy!" Frank said, pulling his plate away, grinning. "If ye wanted chicken, then ye should have ordered it. Speaking of chicken, how's Paul doing?"

Ms. Loy gave him a whimsical smile and returned to watching Rachel and Ryoji dance. They were really into electro swing, with music by Caravan Palace, Caro Emerald, and Alice Francis.

Ms. Loy had to admit that this was the most fabulous wedding she had ever attended. Even the music these two had chosen was gender bent, a rousing fusion of vintage swing, jazz, and hip hop. As Ms. Loy tapped her foot with the beat, she entertained thoughts of getting Mr. McPherson out onto the dance floor. However, her train of thought derailed when she heard the Bishop Able mention Paul.

"He's still completely unrepentant." The Bishop told him as he poked at his food. "I've tried to counsel him, but his hate runs deep. He needs help. I...I actually pity him. He won't let go of his bitterness. He truly believes that he's done nothing wrong and that all this is Rachel's fault. God must deal with him."

"Personally, I always thought he was a little creepy." Ms. Loy admitted.

Mr. McPherson nodded in agreement, still incredulous of Paul's actions and of his own misjudgment of character. "He's excellent at writing horror and mystery. It's why I chose him.

I still can't bring mahself tae believe that he murdered Victoria Cross."

"In his mind, Victoria was sleeping with you, and that's why she was your favorite." The Bishop said, casting his eyes down to the floor. He remembered that he had accused Mr. McPherson of the same thing with Ms. Loy. "He has...serious issues."

Ms. Loy's eyes widened in shock, but before she could speak, Mr. McPherson spoke up. "That's preposterous! Victoria Cross was the most talented playwright that I've ever come tae know. She had an eye fur detail and was an excellent people person. She would have been the greatest Broadway producer ever known, greater than even me. I would never be so brazen as tae disrespect mah employees. I wonder where he got that idiotic idea. I treated all three of mah protégés the same."

"Yeah, like children." Ms. Loy snickered, her eyes twinkling with mischief. She grinned at Frank, her eyes beaming playfully, as she placed her hand on his. "What?"

Mr. McPherson just raised an eyebrow at her and chuckled deeply. "Are ye suggesting that I spoiled them?"

"Oh no, no, no. I'm just. saying that one was a workaholic, the other one is a juvenile, and the wee little one is just insane." Ms. Loy declared, and she took a sip of her drink. "You might want to start giving psych exams with your writing contests."

Mr. McPherson just gawked at Ms. Loy and chuckled. "Ye've been hanging out with Rachel too much." Ms. Loy just giggled at him.

"Speaking of Rachel," The Bishop interjected, his voice full of seriousness and worry. "Paul believes her to be the blame for all his misfortune. He's convinced that she stole his opportunity. He said that she wouldn't even be in the theater if it weren't for him. He's angry that she's so childish and that her plays are so funny. He believes she's laughing at him. He thinks that she is sabotaging him, and he has sworn to get even with her."

"That'll be hard tae do, git even, I mean. He's in prison awaiting trial. I don't believe a jury will let him off with all of the evidence against him. Since this county still believes in capital punishment, he'll most likely be sentenced tae death," considered Mr. McPherson, deep in thought for a moment. He seemed to run scenarios through his mind, and then Ms. Loy poked him to bring him back to earth. "Personally, I think death is far too good fur Paul."

"Amen," Ms. Loy agreed, accepting a piece of wedding cake from the waiter. Mr. McPherson's had been delicious, and she wanted some more.

"But he believes God'll vindicate him, because both Victoria and Rachel were sinners with no morals," Said the Bishop, sipping at his champagne.

"I'm beginning tae think he needs a psychiatrist, nae a cleric." Mr. McPherson commented, now sitting back in his chair to be more relaxed.

"He needs a cat," James said, running his hands along Mr. Tabby's smooth back.

Ms. Loy, Mr. McPherson, Bishop Able, and Mary just looked at him.

"What?" James blushed and coughed to his embarrassment. "Cats are good listeners, and cat people aren't murderers. It would have helped him eliminate some of that anger...my buddy, Mr. Tabby, helped me get over Alex. Didn't you?"

The cat just meowed and purred in agreement as James stroked his cat behind its ears.

"Are all of Rachel's friends this weird?" The fear and morbid grimace on the bishop's face was convincing.

"I'm afraid so," Frank laughed. He lit a cigar, grateful that Rachel had been kind enough to book a hall that allowed smoking. He took a puff and let the smell of his cigar relax him even more. "She has a colorful menagerie o' friends. But if ye think her friends are bad, I can't wait until ye meet Mac's."

Ms. Loy placed a hand over her mouth and started laughing. Frank and Bishop Abel looked at her, but both of them decided not to pursue the matter.

"Hey Rachel! How about letting Ryoji lead fur a while?" Mr. McPherson ordered, as he puffed on his cigar.

Ryoji grinned, slightly embarrassed, and Rachel switched stances. Laughing at each other, they just continued dancing. Spinning, twirling, and wrapping around each other's bodies; moving not as two people, but as two halves of a whole that fit together perfectly.

"That's better." The Bishop chuckled as he continued to watch them dance. "Now the hairs on my neck can go back to sleep."

"Bishop Able?" James called to get his attention.

The bishop turned to face James and his purring pet. "Yes, James."

"I have to go to church once a month, right?" James sought to confirm as he stroked and petted his furry companion.

"Yes, that was the deal." Bishop Able nodded, then he narrowed his eyes on James. "You will honor it."

"Okay right. But does it have to be this church?" James asked, timidly hiding behind his cat.

"Do you have another church in mind?" questioned the Bishop.

"Yes. You see, there is a church, not far from my house, with this young priest whose philosophy is..."

James didn't finish. Bishop Able jumped up from his seat and grabbed James by his collar, but Frank stood and held the Bishop at bay before he could pull James out of the chair.

"That's not a church. It's a cult!. Don't...!" Bishop Able warned James.

"Aw, come on, Steven, the little fella was just teasing you. Weren't you James?" Frank's tone was heavy, and even James could sense the threat. He knew what his answer had better be.

"Yeah, whatever." James was gasping in near panic. His eyes were round, and he kept tapping his heart with his hands, probably trying to make it stop thumping.

"Lord, give me strength." Bishop Able sighed heavily. He sat back down, pinched the bridge of his nose, and wondered how he was supposed to save this man.

His wife Mary smiled and patted her husband's back in sympathy. "Don't worry, dear. It will be alright. They've since closed that church and arrested some of its members for theft and money laundering."

"Hm, Tide and offering." James began laughing as his mind began to race with what kind of church this church had been. One hand covered his mouth, and the other rested against his chuckling stomach. "Where your wallet gets a baptism instead of you."

"Frank, sometimes I think you are a little too forgiving," Bishop Able said, not taking his eyes off James, as he sat back down.

Frank smiled and took a puff of his cigar. *Maybe Bishop was right ... but people deserved the benefit of the doubt occasionally, right?* "Perhaps Steven, but the bible my Mother used tae smack me upside my head with, taught us tae turn the other cheek."

"It teaches to turn the other cheek, true enough," Bishop Able said, adjusting his suit's tie. "But do not turn a blind eye. No stealing is the eighth commandment."

James began to speak, but when he saw Frank and Bishop looking at him, he smiled pleasantly, turned around, and ordered another Perrier from the waiter.

"He was not," argued Sarah, as she danced with Mackenzie. She felt like she was floating…like the ring on her hand made her weightless.

"Ernst Roehm was too." Mackenzie retorted as he gently guided her across the dance floor.

"He was not. He was the head of Hitler's SA Storm Troopers and one of Hitler's staunchest supporters. He wasn't gay. Name one gay murderer." Sarah demanded of him.

"I can name you three books and ask you to read his personal journals. He even had a theme song. Name one straight man with a theme song."

"He had a theme song?" Sara laughed as Mackenzie spun her, letting her swing from his grip.

"Yes. Want to hear it?" Mackenzie gave her a wicked grin.

"Oh, this I've got to hear." She told him as she spun back to his side.

"Zit on mine face und tell me dat you love me. I'll zit on your face und tell you dat I love you too. I love to 'hear you oralize while I'm between you're…," Mackenzie sang, in his best thick German accent.

"MAC!" Sarah screamed with laughter as she purposely stepped on his foot.

"Ouch!" Mackenzie winced and wiggled his foot in pain. He pouted like a kicked puppy as he danced her in circles. "That was unduly harsh, Dr. Able."

"She is going to have her hands full with him," Ryoji laughed, thinking of all the trouble Mackenzie was in for now.

"Aw, don't worry about her. I'm sure she can handle Mac." Rachel smirked. She enjoyed knowing that Sarah could handle Mackenzie's sense of humor well.

Suddenly, Ryoji noticed the Bishop stand up angrily and then sit back down in smoldering contempt.

"I wonder what that's all about?" Ryoji urged Rachel to look in the direction of the reception head table.

Rachel looked and started laughing. "Knowing James, he probably told the Bishop that God is a cat, or something just as bad."

Ryoji burst out laughing so hard that his stomach began to hurt.

"You know, I just thought of a great new play." Rachel smiled at Ryoji as thoughts began to entertain her mind. "One about James and Paul."

"Paul?" Ryoji missed a step as his shock made him stop. But Rachel, without missing a beat, once again took to leading. "The same Paul that almost ruined your career before it started, that Paul?"

"Yeah, something between Milton's Paradise Lost and the Prodigal Son. A story of two brothers, one of damnation and one of redemption."

Ryoji looked at Rachel. He swore he could hear the wheels in her mind turning. "Heh, heh, only you would think like that."

Rachel just laughed at his confusion. "Remember, Ryoji, all the world's a stage, my love," began Rachel.

"And the men and women are merely players," finished Ryoji. "So, is this a comedy or a tragedy?" Ryoji smirked and gave her a wink.

"We are definitely a comedic tragedy." Rachel laughed, spinning Ryoji and pulling him closer to her.

Suddenly, Ryoji stopped dancing. He stared into Rachel's eyes and sighed. This woman, this amazing tomboy, was now and forever his alone. Finally, after so many years of pain, sorrow, and regret, he was so full of love that he thought he would burst. Rachel noticed his gaze.

"And what's wrong with you?" She inquired with a chuckle.

"Wrong? No, for the first time in my life since I was ten years old, everything is right." Ryoji's smile was as bright as the spring day sun.

"You worry too much." Rachel smiled. Her cheeks couldn't puff with any more happiness. So much love did she have for him that she felt as if she would burst like a piñata at any moment.

"Rachel Sato, I love you," Ryoji told her, closing the distance even further between them. Their lips met, and fire surged through them both as Ryoji kissed her passionately, deeply, and truly.

The good Bishop looked up at them, cocked his head to the left, and raised an eyebrow. "Why does this seem so familiar?"

Mr. McPherson and Ms. Loy looked over the dance floor and saw Ryoji and Rachel kissing. Both of them burst out laughing, and Mr. McPherson just patted the shoulder of his oldest and dearest friend.

"Let it go, Steven. Just let it go."

About the Author

Tracy Carol Taylor is a freelance writer, poet, children's e-book author, and young adult novelist. She holds a degree in English and Liberal Arts from Northern Virginia Community College and a degree in English from George Mason University.

Tracy Taylor served in the United States Army for four years. She currently lives in Arlington, VA, with her family. She enjoys reading, writing, video games, and watching movies.

Of Plays, Pals, and Pointless Mayhem